ONCE IN ORDINARY TIME

Published by Christmas Lake Press 2023

www.christmaslakecreative.com

ISBN 978-1-960865-09-0

Interior layout by Daiana Marchesi

ONCE IN ORDINARY TIME

Barbara Walter Hetler

CHRISTMAS LAKE PRESS

For my grandmother and grandfather
who went west on the Homestead Act

Also by Barbara Walter Hetler
Wand Hill

Acknowledgments

I am grateful to the members of the Wesley Writers
Group for their encouragement and support:
Sharon and Steve Fiffer, Christine, Francie, Joyce, Katy,
Kendra, Sarah. And to Tom Fiffer, my publisher, whose
patience, intelligence, humor, and kindness are yet to be
matched—a heartfelt thank you.

Contents

Prologue   i

Early Spring 1904   1

Spring 1904   7

Late Spring 1904   53

Summer And Fall 1904   85

Winter 1904-1905   99

Late Winter 1905   121

Spring 1905   137

Epilogue 1974   163

PROLOGUE

ON THE WESTERN PLAINS, in late summer of 1835, a wooden cradleboard leaned against the trunk of a lone White Oak. In it an infant slept, shaded by the tree's low-hanging branches and soothed by the whispering sound of the wind passing through its leaves.

At dusk a medicine man, traveling as a trusted healer for tribes across the West, stopped to water his horse at a stream near the tree. He was a tall, strong-muscled man who years before had suffered harsh testing with other braves vying for the honored position of tribal leader.

His clothes were sewn from deerskin. Small feathers decorated the sides of each pant leg. Larger ones wound through two dark braids that fell to his shoulders. Simple beaded moccasins sheathed his feet. His side-belt held a skin pouch that he filled with water from the stream, taking a long drink before replacing it.

Before turning the pony out to graze, he removed a blanket and satchel from the animal's back, placing them on the ground beneath the tree's low limbs. As he arranged his resting place, the infant came awake. For a time it was quiet, but after a while it began to make soft cooing noises. Startled, the Indian turned and for a long moment stared at the cradle-bound child reaching out its small hands and arms toward him. He looked around. Not hearing or seeing anyone else, he walked closer.

A girl!

Next to the cradleboard a tiny dress lay folded. When the medicine man picked it up, he found it was of the softest deer hide, made supple until it would be just right against tender skin. Across the collar and hem several butterflies had been sewn. He carefully lifted the baby from the wooden frame that held her.

She did not cry but smiled and grabbed for his hair. Her grip was tight, and she pulled until the Indian laughed.

A distinct odor told him she had soiled herself. Carrying her, he walked to the stream, dipped her into the cool water, then returned to the Oak where he wrapped her in a cloth from his satchel and set her on his blanket.

The spoiled moss lining the inside of the cradleboard needed to be changed. The man tore fresh greenery from the edges of the stream and replaced the old moss as he had seen many Indian mothers do.

After everything was prepared, he picked up the child and gently rocked her in his arms, all the while speaking in soft whispers. When she fell asleep, he tucked her back into the frame.

Not knowing how long the baby had been left under the tree or when she could possibly have eaten last, he wondered if she should be fed soon. He guessed she was about six months old and would probably be able to swallow most softened foods. The herbs in his satchel wouldn't do, but then he remembered the gift of yams given to him by the Yakima tribe. When cooked and mashed they would be perfect.

While the baby slept, the Indian gathered brush and dead branches then started a fire. When it began to smoke, he added a small circle of stones and placed the yams among them, covering all with a flat rock. The strong heat would cook the food quickly.

In no time the yams became soft enough to remove from the fire. The Indian skinned and prepared them, and then went back to the child, who had awakened. She watched as he took a spoon and bowl from his satchel and, kneeling, dipped small amounts of the mashed yams from the bowl. He was pleased when after the first bite she opened her mouth for more.

After she had eaten, he lifted her from the cradleboard. In a soothing voice he told her tales of where he had been until she leaned her head against his chest and fell asleep once more.

The medicine man had been visiting tribes across the Western Plains for several months. Now that the nights lay cooler around him, he wanted to move along quickly. The weather could change without warning. Yet now he felt he must stay at the tree for a while. Someone might come to claim the baby.

Three days and nights passed. No one came. He needed to move on.

Knowing he must take the child with him, he was certain his journey would be more difficult though not impossible. The cradleboard could hang snugly against his back, and, having watched tribal women with their young, he knew what the baby's needs would be. He reasoned that when he stopped at the next village he would ask if anyone had heard of this lost infant.

When the sun rose on the fourth morning, the Indian extinguished the cooking fire and packed his satchel, blanket, and water pouch. In a cloth bundle he wrapped what he would need for the child, tied it to the pony's flank, then placed the baby in the cradleboard securely against his back. Finally, he hoisted himself onto the animal.

As they rode from the Oak, he became aware of a soft fluttering noise. Trying to locate the unusual sound, his eyes were finally drawn to the top of the tree. There, among the canopy, hundreds and hundreds of white butterflies hovered above the leaves, beams of sunlight outlining their transparent wings. When the Indian stopped to watch, the baby spoke in delighted gurgles, reaching her wiggling fingers toward the sky.

Then, having delayed longer than intended, the Indian nudged his pony forward.

He followed the same trails west that he had followed for years, pausing during the day only to attend to the child and rest the pony. Each night they sheltered near a stream. And always the sound of whirring wings spread across the sky—white butterflies—following, stopping only when the man and child did.

For weeks the two journeyed, visiting several villages. The medicine man would then tell of finding the baby at the old Oak, but no one had heard of a lost infant.

As the months passed, he was beginning to feel as if the child belonged to him. At first he had thought he would leave her with one of the tribes, but in his heart, he had come to a place where he could not give her up. And it was then that he named her— Sewana.

The medicine man and Sewana traveled together for years, back and forth across the plains to the many Indian villages. As the child grew, the medicine man taught her more and more about the power of nature and herbs used for healing among their people. When she became a woman, the tribes called her "Medicine Woman... Daughter of the Holy One."

Eventually, the Indian became an old man. It was time for him to go where his life would end in peace. His final stop would be the pine forests and mountains at the end of the western trail—a hidden burial cave where people of many tribes had gone before.

For their final farewell, the woman and he sat beside each other under the ancient White Oak where their story had first begun. During a certain season of the year, the white butterflies still came and rested on the treetop. The gentle words of the old medicine man mixed with the soft whirring sounds in the canopy above.

"I am saddened. But though I leave you now, I will know you again one day. Take what you have learned to our people."

And with that he stood then rode off, leaving Sewana behind to take his place.

EARLY SPRING 1904

THE THUNDERSTORM WAS POWERFUL: lightning, torrential downpour, temperature dropping as the storm's strength grew... then came hail— solid ice the size of a silver dollar—falling with the speed of a galloping mare. Windowpanes were dashed to pieces, sod house wet and peppered with holes, crops battered, and yet another year to wait before replanting.

My parents read of the Homestead Act, a provision where 160 acres of land in the western U.S. could be purchased for $1.25 an acre. This was their chance—a chance at a new life in a new state where they'd triple their acreage. Together they decided to move west to Washington.

The letter Father wrote to a distant cousin who lived outside of Ritzville, a man he'd never met, went something like this:

Dear Ned,

Hope all is well with you.

We are distant cousins who have never met but have heard of you through our friend Sam Forrest who knew you as a boy way back in the old country. Hear you are a grown man now with several grandchildren. What a blessing.

I'm certain you have heard there has recently been much trouble here in Streeter, with bad weather and damaging hail. Our farm has suffered much, and because of this we have decided to move to Washington State. The Homestead Act offers acreage at $1.25 an acre for up to 160 acres. We find this reasonable.

Our thought is, perhaps our son Jonathan might come to stay with you for a short time while he searches for suitable land. We would then come to Ritzville after we settle things here in Streeter. (Of course we would pay for his boarding while he stays with you.) This arrangement would help us to move as soon as possible.

Jonathan is smart, reads well, is good with numbers, and knows much about farming. He is a fine young man, easy to get along with, and quite grown up for a boy of 12.

We are hoping that you will help him until we come West. Let us know if this is acceptable.

Frederick and Katherina Schwartz

Box 10, Streeter, North Dakota

P.S. Please enroll him in the nearest school.

A letter came to our farm within weeks:

Frederick and Katherina,

Glad you wrote me. Knew Sam Forrest when we were boys, way back when. Doubt he'd recognize me now.

Sorry to hear about the damage at your place in Streeter. I have plenty of space here at my home near Ritzville, so Jonathan is more than welcome. My farm is small but he can help with the crops. I am happy to enroll him in the nearest school, as well as help him find Homestead land in the area for your family.

Looking forward to having some company around the place. Will meet him at Ruff, one train stop before Ritzville.

Let me know when he will arrive.

Ned

What follows is the story, as I remember it, of my adventure across the plains, the one that led me from my secure home life in Streeter, North Dakota to one that was beyond my wildest imagination.

My name is Jonathan Schwartz. My parents sent me to Old Ned in spring 1904.

SPRING 1904

T HEY STOOD ON THE platform as the train pulled
away, Father still as stone, Mother's hands
cupped over her eyes, my little sister waving.
With my face pressed against the window, I watched as
they grew smaller and finally disappeared.

I was headed to Ruff, Washington, a small town east
of Ritzville, where the train would make a special stop
just for me. I would be the only one getting off. My dad
said I was going there "on business," making me feel more
like a man than a boy of twelve.

I was assured Cousin Ned would meet me at the
station and we'd be going to his farm between Ruff and
Ritzville. Though none of us had ever met the man, the
thought that I would be staying with family was a relief.
I wouldn't be alone.

But as the train rolled farther and farther from
Streeter, the feeling of becoming a man began to fade,

and my courage started melting into uncertainty. I sat thinking of the home I had just left, blinking at tears that threatened. Then I thought of my father's words, "Pull yourself up by the bootstraps, son," and a warm strength surged through me.

I saw my face outlined in the window, my brown eyes staring back at me. My hair had been cut short the day before, Father using Mother's sewing scissors and dropping the clipped pieces into a bowl on our kitchen table. I was already missing the mass of brown curls I once had.

My face reflected my thoughts. "Search out 160 acres of Homestead land," my father had said. "Have Cousin Ned send a telegram letting us know when we should leave for Washington." The responsibility made me feel weak.

This was my first train ride. The engine belched black smoke, cinders, and steam while the wheels beat a music-like rhythm on the tracks below. Through the wide-glassed window, the prairie flew past, the stark land of the plains stretching for miles. Here and there a sod house, a barn, a windmill plunked down in the middle of nowhere. Their world seemed isolated and lonely.

Few passengers were in my train car, so I had a double seat all to myself. The straw suitcase sitting next to me held a few items of clothing, a family picture, a journal, and money from my father sewn into its lining. A canteen of water, a small sack holding two apples and a loaf of my mother's homemade bread lay beside it. I kept my few possessions close so they wouldn't be snatched by a stranger.

For two days and nights we travelled. Though we made short stops once or twice at stations, I was afraid to leave the train. At night I barely slept, constantly aware of my surroundings, believing the ride was the most dangerous part of my journey.

The skies had stayed clear until we reached Ruff where a sudden storm surrounded us. It swept over the train, rattling windows and leaving thin streams of water spilling down the glass. I was reminded of the hail that had ruined our lives in Streeter, but, not hearing the banging of that ice against the train's roof, I felt my racing heart slow. Soon I'd be on my way to Cousin Ned's. I had kept my poncho next to me, using it as a blanket during the trip, and now slipped it over my head to protect me from the rain I was about to face.

Leaving behind the emptied sack that now only held two apple cores and a few breadcrumbs, I shouldered my canteen, grabbed my suitcase, and stepped off the train onto the station platform. As I stood there alone, I watched the glow of the brakeman's lantern wave back and forth signaling the train to move on.

The night was cool, windy, darker than dark. Through the downpour I could make out a weathered wooden sign, "Welcome to Ruff," as it swung and creaked in the wind that whirled around the empty station house. Faint light from two station lamps reflected off a dented water tank tipping eerily toward the tracks. Near it someone stood in the shadows.

"Cousin Ned?" I called out, hoping it was him.

As he moved toward me, the lamps outlined a skinny man about a head taller than I was. He wore an old boot-length coat, the bottom frayed, the sleeves torn. A black beard trailed over the coat collar. The worn hat that hung low over his eyes dripped rain from its wide brim in a steady stream to the ground. A canteen was tipped to his lips.

"Cousin Ned," I said again.

He lowered the canteen, spit, swiped his mouth with one sleeve, then turned my way and squinted.

"Jonathan Schwartz?"

"I am," I said, walking toward him and extending my hand.

He took mine and shook it. His grip was tight as a vice.

"Didn't 'spect ya ta be so small," he said. "How old you say you was?"

"Twelve."

"Scrawny for bein' twelve."

"They tell me I'm average for my age," I said, feeling suddenly smaller than I was.

"Well, no use standin' round here chattin' boy. Might as well be goin'. Dark night, long trail," he said as we stood face to face. His breath was stale, the rank odor heavy from whatever it was he was chugging. "We're gonna have ta ride together. Wagon broke down. No time ta fix it afore you come."

He turned and walked away, signaling me to follow to the back of the station house. There one pitiful looking horse stood, head down, ears flattened, soaked blanket in place of a saddle.

"Name's Ellie," Ned said, giving the animal a slap on the muzzle. He took another swig from the canteen then mounted the horse. Weighed down by my belongings, I struggled to hoist myself up.

"Don't hold that stuff too close to her hindquarters," Ned said sharply. "She spooks easy."

I kept my canteen shouldered and wedged the suitcase between us, leaving little room for two riders. Ned gave Ellie a sharp kick to the belly, and we started out at a lumbered walk, the horse side-stepping now and then around puddles.

"Rain like this all the time?" I asked, my voice loud enough to be heard over the storm.

"Sagebrush country... mostly dry round here," he shouted back. After that he was quiet, concentrating on what was ahead and on drinking from that canteen of his. In the endless dark I couldn't make out the sage or much of anything else for that matter. Moisture soaked my pants and ran down the insides of my boots, but because of the poncho, my head and upper body stayed dry. We rode in silence, on and on, Ned weaving a bit as the horse moved along, me nodding off so often that I had no memory of the journey's length or of what direction we had taken.

The sound of Ned's boots hitting the ground as he dismounted jarred me awake. I sat up straight for a moment, not able to remember where I was. An afternoon sun was low in the sky and rain from the night before had left the sweet scent of sage in the air. Ned had tied Ellie to a stake near a broken-down wagon and was yelling at me to get off the horse. I slid clumsily off the animal's back, my suitcase in one hand, my empty canteen over one shoulder.

"I'd offer you some of this, but it ain't the right stuff for a boy," he said, tipping his canteen to his lips. Not finding a drop left, he shook it upside down to prove to himself that it was empty.

"You thirsty... drink from that." He pointed to a wooden barrel near the horse's stake.

I lifted the dipper from a hook on the barrel's side and took a long drink. The water tasted of dust, but my thirst was so great it didn't matter.

Having expected Ned's house to be made of sod or wood, I was surprised to follow him to a dirt dugout in the side of a hill, its opening covered with an animal's skin. He pushed the skin aside, grabbed a kerosene lamp from inside the doorway, struck a match on the sole of his boot, and lit the wick.

"Home sweeter 'n sweet home," he slurred.

The faint light flickered over two tree stump seats, a splintered table, and a stack of wooden boxes. Plant roots poked through the dirt ceiling overhead. A pile of animal hides lay on the floor. I guessed this to be his bed, while mine would probably be the mound of worn blankets dumped in a far corner. The whole room smelled of sweat, must, and something rotting.

Two holders jammed in the dirt wall held chipped glass hurricane chimneys covering half-burned candles. Ned lit these and the dim room filled with light. I could see the entire place now and what I saw my mind could hardly take in.

The flickering candlelight spread then spilled off the hairs of dozens of wolf hides and puppy pelts—grey, black, silver—that hung on the walls. In the light each coat glistened with a silky sheen. A collection of paws hung on ropes from the ceiling. The sight made me feel ill.

Somewhere I found my voice. "You kill wolves!"

"You bet," he sneered. "Trap 'em. Sounds a heap better than kill, eh? Ugly creatures. Mean. I do everybody a favor. Big money in wolf hides. Keeps me in this." He held up the empty canteen.

"But there are pup pelts up there too!"

"My thought is wipe 'em out any ol' way you can afore they grow and breed."

With that he moved to the stack of boxes, reached inside one, and brought out some strips of beef jerky and a couple of apples. After laying the food in the middle of the table, he left the dugout, returning only moments later.

"Like I told ya, get yer own drink from that wood barrel outside. I got mine here." He patted the canteen, tipped it to his mouth, and took a long swallow. I wondered where he had gone to refill it.

"Let's eat," he grunted.

We shoved the tree stumps against the table. The jerky was heavily salted, more so than I was used to back home. The apples were mushy, close to rotting. While we ate, neither of us spoke, yet my mind was full of questions.

At the station I'd been happy to see Ned. Though my family had never met him, we had been told he was a distant cousin who'd done well for himself in Washington. But this man, the way he looked, the way he behaved, wasn't at all what I'd expected. In fact, nothing that had happened so far was what I had imagined it to be. Where was his farm? The house he'd written about in his letter?

Perhaps he had fallen on hard times, I reasoned. After all, that had happened to our family in Streeter. What I had experienced so far had made me want to ask him straight out, to alleviate my doubts.

Yet I found I didn't have the courage.

After we had eaten, he got up from the table, "You sleep over there," he said, pointing to the mound of crumpled blankets. Then he stumbled to the bed of hides and, holding the canteen tightly against his chest, fell full out on his back and instantly began to snore.

That night I spent in and out of sleep, tossing on a pile of filthy, tattered blankets. My suitcase, still unpacked, sat on the floor next to me. Although we had eaten the apples and jerky, I still felt hunger growing deep in my belly. The stuffy air in the place made me sneeze. I longed for home.

A few hours of restless sleep were all I had before awakening. The candles had burned down, and the only light coming in was from holes in the door's skin. When my eyes finally adjusted, I saw the crude furnishings again: the horror of wolf and pup pelts on the walls and the paws hanging from the ceiling. I shook my head, hoping it was all a dream.

I called for Ned, and when he didn't answer, I scrambled from my makeshift bed and walked out of the dugout. He had taken Ellie and was gone! My mouth was dry, so I went to the water barrel and took several gulps, then I looked up at the open sky. It was a quiet dawn, only a slight breeze. With its lonely distant song, a bird let me know the day had begun.

I looked across the prairie from one horizon to the next—miles and miles of wild, dry land without any sign of another living being. Nothing but dusty, grey sagebrush growing here and there in disorderly clumps. Several bushes clung to the ground against the dugout. I rubbed a few small leaves between my fingers, and a musty yet not unpleasant smell filled my nose. I tugged at one bush then another. The first came out of the ground easily while the second wouldn't budge. It was difficult to break the bush and its woody stem down with my hands.

Father had been told it would be easy to clear this land. It didn't look to be so. Too rugged. How could he ever make a living here? Maybe we'd be making a mistake leaving the Dakotas. I thought of writing, sending a telegram. But how could I get a message to him? I had no idea where I was and had a strange feeling Ned wouldn't help me out.

I went back inside the dugout, opened my suitcase, and took out my journal. When I began to read, I saw I'd only written two new pages—those on the train before I had reached Ruff. Nothing since.

And so I began, describing my meeting this man at the station stop, his unusual appearance, the dugout where he lived, the wolf pelts. I had been anticipating an exciting adventure when I first began heading west. Now I wasn't so sure where this was headed.

I wrote of my feelings and found myself longing for home again. Closing the journal at last, I laid it under my blankets where it would stay hidden, especially from Ned.

Ned returned that afternoon riding in on Ellie. His matted hair hung from under his hat to his shoulders. His face was dark and lined from being in the sun, his greasy beard long and unkempt. He wore a dirty long-sleeved wool undershirt with holes in the elbows, and his bibbed overalls were stained, torn at the knees, and frayed around his dusty boots. One dark bloody wolf pelt was tied over the horse's rump.

"Rotten day," he grumbled, took the hide, and threw it at me. He slid from the horse, tied her to the stake, and walked my way. He held a switch in one hand and kept smacking it against one leg.

"Show ya once how ta clean a hide," he barked. "From now on you'll do it alone. Took care of skinnin' her out when I trapped her. Scraped off the flesh and fat. Left her innards in the woods, 'cept for the brains." He raised the switch above his head and brought it down hard against the ground, making me jump sideways.

He went to the back of the broken-down wagon where a large pan, small wooden table, drying rack, and large metal tub lay inside. After lifting everything out he told me to drag the tub to the trough and fill it with water.

"Git some soap, some matches, and twine from the dugout, boy. They're in the box marked 'Tannin'."

I did as he asked, afraid if I didn't that switch would be used on me.

"Now yer gonna wash this here hide with water and soap 'til all the dirt an' blood is gone... every last bit of it."

He added the soap then plunged the hide into the tub. "Git over here boy and swish this round 'til it come clean. An' pay attention... you'll be doin' the work from now on."

Ned watched me for a while, telling me to push hard, rub until I couldn't feel my fingers, then he went behind the dugout and came back with an armful of dried wood. He stacked that, lit a small fire, set the pan of water on top, and reached for a thick mass of what looked like lumpy fat that lay in a bowl nearby.

"Boil the water then add these wolf brains I brung home. Stir it 'til it looks like soup."

The mixture smelled putrid, and I felt ill just working with it.

After a while, he removed the pan to let it cool. When I went back to scrubbing the wolf hide, he set up the drying rack.

I'd seen one of these in Streeter used by an old trapper who lived miles from town. Once I'd ridden out to his place, snuck up, and watched him. I'm sure he knew all along I was there, but never let on. He'd had everything for tanning at his fingertips and worked several hides at a time, making certain all the steps he took were perfect. These skins he'd sell to people who'd pay big cash to own one. It occurred to me, then, that maybe I'd want to be a trapper someday. But now I was having a change of heart.

Pulling me back from my thoughts, I heard Ned shout, "Move along now, boy. You take that hide out o' the water an' squeeze it good."

The skin was incredibly heavy. I pulled it over one side of the tub and pressed down with my hands so that much of the water could run out. Then, with as much strength as I could gather, I began squeezing the hide with my entire body.

"Bring it here," Ned commanded after a while. But because the hide was still wet, it was difficult to carry the weight by myself.

With a lot of grumbling, he helped me lift the skin, carry it to the back of the wagon, and lay it out flat. After, he punched holes around the pelt edges, wound twine through these, and together we stretched it onto the drying rack.

"Now yer gonna dip into that there brain soup you been stirrin'. Take out half the brains and mash them into this here skin with yer bare hands 'til it's nice and soapy." He tipped the rack, hide and all, against the wooden table and handed me the pan.

"Do it! Jus' like I told ya! An' rub that stuff deep. Keep it up 'til you feel the pelt drying. Then do it again, same as before!"

The mess in the pan made me swallow hard to keep from being sick.

"That's one ugly face yer makin'. Are you a man or just a whiny little boy?" he sneered.

His words were making me feel small. Was I just a whiny little boy after all?

Then I thought of my father, who had such faith in me when I left Streeter. His words came to me again.

"Pull yourself up by your bootstraps, son." And I felt a sudden burst of courage.

No way was I going to let Ned know how I felt. I clenched my teeth and, with both hands, reached into the pan, scooped out a handful of the mixture, and rubbed it deep into the bare side of the pelt. Each time I pressed harder until the skin on my hands and arms was raw.

Ned went to the dugout and brought out a couple of thin blankets. He dipped them in the trough then spread them over the bare side of the hide.

"This'll set overnight," he said. "When the hide dries, we'll smoke it."

Before I came awake the following morning, and even before the sun was up, Ned had removed the blankets from the pelt, built a campfire of rotten wood, and hung the skin over the teepee-like structure where the fire could smolder and smoke the hide. Later, with a lot of shouting, he made me carry the hide and drape it over the wagon's side, where the heat from the sun would dry it completely. He kept calling me a "lazy-good-for-nothing" and, although he'd give me water, refused me anything to eat that entire day.

After several days of drying, he brought the hide into the dugout and nailed it to a wall. Though I had worked hard preparing that pelt, I felt no satisfaction in destroying an animal whose only desire was to live out her life roaming the wilderness.

Nothing good ever happened between us. At every turn he made me obey, and if I hesitated, he thrashed me with that switch until welts rose on my arms and legs. I desperately wanted to leave but didn't have any idea where I was in this God-forsaken place, so I couldn't take a chance on running away and getting lost.

Ned worked me like a plow horse. Either I did everything he told me to or I paid the price. If no rain filled the barrel, he'd send me a mile to a cistern with a bucket for water. Once, when I was almost to the dugout again, I stumbled. Half of it spilled. He poured the rest on the ground in front of me, and then jammed the bucket back in my hand.

"Go back to the cistern! Fill the bucket to the top. Crawl here if you have to, but don't spill a drop this time or... you'll go back 'til you get it right!"

I'd work the hides and clean the bloodied traps he brought home. I'd dig new toilet holes outside the dugout every day and fill the old ones with dirt. I'd cook, and if it wasn't to his liking, he'd throw the meal outside the hut, onto the ground, and tell me to clean it up and start again! "Do it boy an' don't give me any lip," he'd growl, holding up his fist.

I lived in fear of what he might do next. The way he treated me, every word he spoke, seemed like a threat. The search for a 160-acre homestead was never mentioned. Enrolling me in school was never brought up. To my knowledge he had never written my parents to let them know where I was. It seemed I myself had almost begun to forget who I was. And I was beginning to think that maybe Ned and I were not related.

The days seemed long yet scrambled together. To keep from giving up, I'd tell myself to stay strong, someone would surely find me. At night I'd dream of running away, yet the next morning that always seemed impossible.

One night after drinking an entire canteen of whatever made him stumble around, Ned demanded I bring him my suitcase. I had kept it next to my bed, covered with a blanket, hoping he would forget about it. There was no way I wanted him to find out about the money hidden in the lining.

"There's nothing in my suitcase but some clothes and a family picture."

He was sitting at the table. "Bring it here!" he demanded, his words slurring.

Dumping the contents on the floor near his feet, he stood and kicked the pile around. "Just a bunch o' clothes," he grumbled.

"Like I said..."

His face turned purple as he lurched toward me. "Sassin' me boy?" He shoved the clothes to one side with his foot.

"Well, looky here... will ya jus' look at that... a tintype of yer maw, paw, you, an'... looks like some scrawny little gal. Yer sister maybe? Now ain't that too sweet."

He grabbed the photo, fingering the edges with his dirty hands, then slammed it down on the table. Next he picked up the suitcase, shook it, and began to feel around the inside.

"Well, well. What's this here?"

The bills had fallen in a lump to the bottom of the lining. He took a knife from his pocket and slashed the fabric.

"You're ruining my suitcase!" I said, hoping he would stop.

"I said, DON'T SASS ME!"

He had reached a hand inside the lining and was pulling out the bundle of cash. "My, my, my. What do we have here? You been keepin' this from me, boy? You been hidin' money on me when ol' Ned is payin' for yer keep all along?"

He fondled the bills, then he shoved the whole wad into his overall bib pocket. "Well now, I'll jus' keep it safe right here," he said, patting his chest.

"But... I'm surely beginnin' to feel like I owe you somethin' in exchange for this here cash. Only fair, I'd say." He stood and moved close enough to me that I could see the wildness in his eyes.

"How 'bout this... I AIN'T NO RELATIVE O' YERS!" He snickered and shoved two fingers hard into my chest.

I stared at him, unable to settle on what he was saying. "But my father... the letter..." The words hardly formed themselves.

"Jus' pure LUCK!!" he chuckled. "Found this here dugout abandoned two years past an' claimed it. Come home from a week a trappin' a few months back an' seen a letter left inside on the table. Some fool must o' walked right in my place, no invite or nothin', an' left it. T'weren't addressed to me but I read it anyways. Someone lookin' for a Ned Schwartz to board his kid. So's I figured, why not! Here's my chance to get me some free help. Save me a lot a sweat."

There had been so many unanswered questions swirling around in my mind, questions I had wanted to ask Ned before this but was afraid to. Now I knew. Ned was not a cousin after all. "Ned" was not Ned. He was a stranger. He was frightening. And now I realized what I had begun to suspect: he treated me the way he did because he wanted someone who could do all his work for him. He hadn't mentioned contacting my parents because he had never intended to. And now he had taken my money. I would never be able to leave. I would have to live here slaving for him until he wore me down completely. I was stranded, alone with this man. My tears welled up, but I didn't dare let him see.

Even though "Ned" had my money, I didn't see any improvement in anything around the place, including meals. It was still pretty much beans, jerky, and apples. Once in a while we spit a hare. Ned would gorge himself, then, whatever was left, I ate. It took a lot of rough nights before my system became used to that kind of eating. And I was getting thinner.

He kept a close eye on me until maybe a month had passed, then he began to leave more often to set his traps. There were times he would not return for several days. It was always the wolves he was after. When he returned, he'd fill his canteen and sit outside the dugout guzzling until he fell asleep for hours. I figured while he was on a hunt, he'd probably bought a gallon of the stuff from some moonshiner and had hidden his supply somewhere near the dugout. When he slept or was gone, I could count on being alone and would spend my time outside wandering. My thoughts continued to weigh on me.

"I have to leave this place. But there's no way out that I can see. Where was that station stop? What direction had we ridden that first night? How far had we gone? Mother and Father haven't heard from me. Surely they must be worried. What should I do next?"

Mid-morning one day, Ned was sprawled alongside the dugout. I had been watching him drink then fall asleep. When he slept, he usually didn't wake for hours. I grabbed the water bucket and my canteen. The path to the cistern was fairly worn by now. Today my idea was to go farther than that, keeping some sort of marker in sight so I could find my way back.

When I reached the cistern, I filled the bucket first then my canteen. Leaving the bucket behind, I began walking westward. My father had taught me to judge the time of day and direction by the sun. Ahead, as far as the horizon, was a dry-grey sea of sagebrush. To keep myself on a definite path I'd decided to bend the larger top branches of the bushes as I went along.

As I continued an old sensation welled up inside me, one I hadn't felt in months. Being away from the confines of the dugout seemed to lift my spirits. I was feeling a freedom that had escaped me since I'd been with Ned. For a while this feeling stayed with me, but after a short time, my sense of freedom started to dwindle and I began to sweat. I thought, is it the sun or the sudden realization that I could get lost, turned around, and not find my way back to the dugout? Or is it because Ned might have come awake and found me gone?

The broken sage branches were well within view, close enough to each other so that it was easier than I'd thought to find my way to the cistern. Once there I grabbed the full bucket and headed back.

Luckily Ned was still asleep. But what if he had come awake? I worried he might suspect what I was doing. But my need to escape this nightmare had begun to overpower my fear.

As the days passed, I became more and more confident. When Ned left to trap, I'd leave for the cistern and places beyond. This time I tied strips of fabric torn from my suitcase lining to the lower parts of the sagebrush as I went along. Each trip took me a little farther.

As I successfully repeated the same trip, my boldness increased. When Ned packed Ellie for several days of hunting and trapping, I chose to venture in a different direction than I'd been going... west and north of the cistern.

I followed the thin strips of fabric until they ended, then, as I pushed forward, added pieces to the bushes that were new to me. I went farther than I had ever gone—I figured at least an hour from the cistern. It was then that I saw the coulee.

I had heard of a coulee when I lived in North Dakota as a streambed that held water people depended upon. This one was bone-dry, caked, and had cracked over the years from dry seasons, little rain, and the heat of the sun.

Where the water had once met the land, thick caps of bush-grass lipped over, hugging the ground above and sending roots that hung like thin hairs over the sides. A slight breeze made them sway. I jumped down into the dry streambed and walked for a while, kicking the clay and crumbling it between my fingers.

Here and there the embankment folded inward, carving out small niches hollowed out by running water from past years. As I moved along, I noticed a few larger openings, one in particular cutting deeper than the others.

I knelt down.

When my eyes adjusted to the darkness, I could see the hole was large enough to hold a skinny boy like me.

I crawled inside.

Twisting about, I found with a little effort I could sit upright, stretch my legs, and lean my back against the dirt wall. At that very moment I made my decision. "I will run away. This will be my first hiding place... a perfect place to rest when I go."

It was a day like most spring days in sage country—dusty, with a slight wind that blew dry tumbleweed and loose sage around like some wild thing. This day there were a few scattered clouds in the sky but nothing that threatened rain.

"Ned" had begun to leave the dugout for even longer periods lately. I supposed it was because he thought he'd put the fear of the devil in me and I wouldn't go anywhere far. I watched as he loaded three traps, a blanket, a sack of food, and his canteen on Ellie. "Another long hunt," I thought.

"Don't do nothin' foolish," he growled, and then, when I turned my back, shoved me to the ground with such force that my chin and hands slid along the rough dirt, and dust went up my nose.

"I mean it!" he barked, climbed atop Ellie, kicked her in the sides, and left. I lay there until I was certain he was gone.

When I finally stood, I was a mess—chin and hands bloodied, dust from head to toe—but my mind was completely clear. This was the time! There was no doubt.

Ignoring my bloody scrapes, within moments I ran to the horse trough and dragged out my poncho that was hidden beneath. An old shirt—stained in wolf blood from the traps I'd been cleaning—strips of fabric from my suitcase, some apples, jerky, a canteen, and my journal were bundled inside.

Grabbing the water bucket, I took off at a run for the cistern. If "Ned" happened to turn back and caught me away from the dugout, my alibi would be that I was just going for water as usual. I ran faster than I had ever run before. Even with the bundle I carried and the bucket swinging by my side, I reached the cistern in record time.

After dipping the bucket, I spilled the contents on the ground then threw it aside. Opening the poncho, I pulled out the bloodied shirt, tore it into shreds, and tossed it over a nearby bush along with my pack. I stuffed the food and strips of fabric into the poncho pockets, tied it around my waist, and slung the canteen over one shoulder. I struggled to pull a sage bush from the ground, but once it was uprooted, I made deep gouges in the dirt and trampled the bushes nearby. I hoped the scene looked like a pack of wild animals had attacked if "Ned" came looking for me.

Now I would never look back.

Because of the pieces of fabric tied to the sage bush, it was easy for me to find the coulee. This time I untied them as I went forward, shoving them into the pockets of my poncho.

By the time I arrived at the coulee's cave, the scattered clouds had started to thicken and the wind was getting stronger. I crawled inside for protection. I was not totally uncomfortable though my head kept hitting the ledge of ground above me. Exhausted but relieved that I had escaped this far, I bent my legs, tipped my neck forward, and rested my forehead on my knees. My eyes closed.

At the sound of something or someone approaching outside, I jerked awake. "Do not be afraid," I told myself over and over. "Do not be afraid."

My thoughts went wild: wolves! Ned! Ned!

I pushed my back against the cave wall and pressed a hand to my mouth. "No sound... don't make a sound!" But the urge to stretch became unbearable. My legs were cramping. I had to get out of this space. I crunched into a ball, rolled out of my hiding place, and peeked over the embankment.

A furious wind had begun to blow. Clouds of loose dust from the dry land surface were rising higher and higher toward the heavens. With a deafening whine it was coming toward me, loosened particles so dense that the sun could not be seen. For miles, it seemed, the dust had become a solid, high wall.

The storm ripped its fury around me, stinging my face, my arms, making it difficult to breathe. The crazed wind attacked the prairie like a wild animal. I scrambled back into the hollow cave hoping it would protect me.

The wind's angry sound seemed to go on forever. Though I covered my ears, I could still hear its roar above, surrounding me, reaching deep into the cave to find me.

Again my legs cramped. Once more I crawled out of the hollow space, covered my face with my hands, and stood. Thinking at first it was the wind throwing me off balance, I fought against it, trying to lower myself into the cave. But the pull became even stronger. I couldn't shake myself loose.

With a sudden quick movement, I was lifted from the ground and in an instant felt the body of a horse beneath me. Because of the dust I couldn't see, but I instinctively reached out to grab something for balance. Blindly, my hands grasped what felt like a shirt.

Breathing was now almost impossible, with dust clogging my nose and mouth. The strong force of the raging wind bit into my skin. My eyes stung. Terrified, I tried to scream but couldn't make a sound. I coughed and choked almost uncontrollably.

The horse lunged and began to run. I clung to the rider in front of me while squeezing my calves and knees tightly against the animal's stomach in order to keep myself upright. With every movement the belly heaved in and out. The wind, heavy with grit, whistled, whining in my ears as we rode at breakneck speed to escape the torture.

Reaching to the sky, spread wide across the plains, a whirling wall enclosed us. Yet the horse drove on, tail flying, mane whipping about. The animal's strained breathing kept time with his pounding hooves.

Just when I thought I might suffocate, we seemed to be heading away from the overpowering force of the storm. The animal's frantic stride slowed, becoming more of an easy rhythm. We continued at this steady pace, the horse moving between a trot and a gallop. On and on we rode, over the flat prairie. The sky was dark. Thunder threatened. Lightning flashed. Yet rain never came.

Though my eyes burned, I could see that the land had begun to change. Ahead of us scrub pines now dimly outlined what appeared to be rocky hills. Reaching their base, the horse began to climb until sparse groves of tall thin pines surrounded us. Black boulders lay on the hills like predators ready to pounce.

The horse moved in a slow, zigzag motion around the huge rocks. I could feel the animal's sweat beneath my trousers as it strained to move up the hill, scrambling for a foothold that would not bring us tumbling down. If the animal lagged for a moment, it would suddenly jerk forward, almost pitching me off its rump. I clung to the rider, fear filling every part of my body.

More and more the land began to roll, opening at times in a clearing then climbing the steep mountainside along a rocky ridge hanging frighteningly close to a canyon. We rode on, the boulders becoming less frequent, the forest more and more dense. Only the thump of the horse's hooves, its heavy breathing, and the faraway sound of rushing water could be heard.

As night came on, the movement of the animal beneath me and the rustle of the wind sifting gently through the trees brought memories of my family and farm far away in Streeter. I thought, "The same stars are looking down on them. The same wind is bending the wheat on the land my father plows. But where are they now? And where am I?"

Visions of home kept unwinding in my mind. So deep in thought was I that when I heard someone say, "Where am I being taken?" and "Home... home is where I want to be," I didn't realize I was the one speaking those words aloud.

We traveled on for hours, pausing now and then to stop for water and to relieve the horse. When we did, I learned that it was an Indian woman who had saved me from the storm.

She was old, her back bent like a willow bough, face creased with age. Yet like someone younger, she moved about quietly in her deerskin clothing, her thick grey braid swinging against her back. In a voice I understood she told me her name was Sewana. I told her mine was Jonathan.

Though I had no idea where we were or where we were headed, I was strangely not afraid. The woman seemed gentle and kind, not at all a threat. My experience with the few Indian families that lived outside Streeter had been good. One of the young boys had taught me how to string a bow. I had traded him some partridge feathers for the lesson.

That first night, we rested in a clearing. She set up camp, taking a blanket from the horse's back and spreading it on the ground. "You will sleep here," she said softly. How different I thought from the harsh words "Ned" used when he told me to sleep on the worn, musty blankets when I first came to the dugout.

Sewana then walked into the dark woods nearby, returning quickly with a bundle of branches. The weather had cooled as we had ridden higher into the mountains, so the small fire she made would keep us warm through the cold night.

When I awoke that next morning, my eyes had become slits, the lids almost closed. My throat was like coarse sand and I coughed constantly, causing my ribs to ache. Though the mountain air was cold and misty, my body felt unbearably hot. Again, I longed for home.

Just as my mother had done when I wasn't well, Sewana laid her hand on my forehead. "You have a high fever," she said. She brought me something to eat, but I couldn't stand the thought of swallowing food yet I craved liquid. She put a cool, wet cloth on my forehead and over and over gave me water from a pouch. Still, there never seemed to be enough to quench my unending thirst.

While I rested, she began erasing any sign that we had been there—dousing the fire and taking a pine bough to rub away any footprints we may have made. With those movements I felt as if part of my young life in North Dakota was also being erased. Would I ever again remember any of it clearly? Would I ever see my family again?

She folded the blanket over the animal's back then helped me mount. With the rope rein she hoisted herself up in front of me. Feeling dizzy and weak, I leaned against her back to steady myself.

We left that first campsite to face the same type of terrain we had traversed: dense forests, meadows, canyons, and streams. We rode on, stopping only briefly once or twice during the day then at night to make camp.

Every evening Sewana would go into the forest, returning with woodland plants that might cure my fever and wood for the evening's fire. There seemed to always be a creek nearby, and she would bring back water, heat it over the flames, and use it to clean the dust and sweat that covered my face and arms.

Because of the ache in my bones, by the third day I could barely sit on the pony. My eyelids had sealed shut and, though my entire body was hot and sweaty, I was constantly shivering. Sewana took the blanket from the animal's back and wrapped it around me. We stopped for water often, for that was the only thing that truly soothed me.

Mostly we rode, but at times both of us had to walk. Sewana would guide the horse around fallen rock, over dead trees, and through streams. I'd stumble along, held upright by Sewana's strong arms.

The fever made me doze, so I was uncertain as to how many days we'd traveled. I was only aware of riding long hours, walking some, and stopping to rest at night.

It felt like we had been on the journey forever. Then suddenly I could hear, could feel the quiet. No breeze, no sound of hooves pounding the ground. I was helped off the pony. I walked unsteadily, trembling all the while, unable to see. Sewana took hold of my hand.

"You are at my dwelling," she said quietly. "The opening is small, so you must bend your knees to enter."

She helped me lower my head and shoulders and then, once inside, asked me to sit. Beneath me I could feel the soft press of pine needles under a smooth animal skin. Sewana handed me a fresh blanket. "Wrap yourself in this," she said. "Lay your clothes here by your bed so that I might clean and dry them by the fire."

I did as she asked, aware of her movements about the dwelling, her footsteps light as a deer's. What my eyes could not see, my nose and ears were telling me. The odor of wood and the warmth of heat had filled the space. Water was being poured. After a few minutes I could hear it boiling and smell the pungent scent of sage in the air.

A warm cloth was placed over my closed lids and tied behind my head. I was reminded of home again… how once, when I was ill, my mother had put churned butter on a rag, held it up to a kerosene lamp, then laid the warmed folded fabric across my forehead. I passed into a dream-like sleep.

Thoughts of family and home swirled in my brain. Was I in Streeter with them or was I now in an altogether different place—one I had never been before? If I was dreaming I was with my family, then what I was going through here and now must actually be real. My high fever was playing games with me.

When I awoke later my dry clothes lay next to my bed. I struggled to stand and put them on, coughing the whole while, my chest feeling like a leather strap had tightened around it. I pulled aside the cloth that covered my eyes, but the lids were still sealed shut. I tried to hold back the tears that were building inside me.

"You must let the wet sage rag soften the crust. Then your eyes will open," Sewana said quietly, in a voice I felt I could trust.

I sat back down, and she placed another warmed damp cloth over my lids. Wrapping my hands around a cup of hot water steaming with the smell of sage she said, "This is a gift from the Earth. It heals the eyes, the throat, the body. Drink. Then lay back. Rest. In time you will be well."

With the strong scent of sage in the room, the warm cloth, and the comfort of the blanket, this time I fell into a deep sleep.

Another day passed before Sewana removed the second cloth from my eyes. I touched my lids, fearing they were still sealed. She gently moved my hands aside. With a moistened cloth, she carefully stroked the loosened crust, then rinsed and patted each lid dry.

"Now," she said. "Open slowly."

I opened my eyes, blinked several times in the light, squinted and strained to view my surroundings. Though my vision was still somewhat blurred, the wet cloth had removed the crust.

"I can see," I said, my voice cracking as I took in everything around me.

The room was round, big enough to hold several people and tall enough to stand in. Woven bark mats covered parts of the smooth dirt floor. Wooden poles painted with dozens of white butterflies supported a dome-shaped roof made from tightly twisted tree branches that extended to the ground.

A thin stream of light shone here and there through the bent boughs along the walls. At one end, a door of branches covered in deerskin led to the outside. Dried plants hung in tied bundles from the circular ceiling. Woven baskets sat along the floor, clay jugs against the walls.

Sewana was tending a slow-burning fire in a small pit in the center of the room. Flames flickered low and blue-orange. Curls of wispy smoke rose, vanishing through a hole in the domed roof. A pot of water sat in the center of the fire, sending off steam, a larger vessel heating alongside.

With a ladle, she dipped into the larger pot, filled a bowl, and handed it to me. Dandelion leaves floated on top of a clear broth. The bottom was heavy with meat I could not identify. I finished every morsel then tipped the bowl to get the last drop of remaining broth. My appetite had returned.

"It is morning... morning of your sixth day," Sewana said.

I couldn't fathom how that much time had passed. Six days? "Where am I?" I asked.

Her eyes, light blue and clear as a morning sky, looked straight at me. Sewana wore leggings, moccasins, and a buckskin dress. Several small white butterflies had been sewn along the dress sleeves. She was quiet for a time.

"The mountains and forest south and west of the plains," she finally said while walking to the fire to refill my bowl. "My home."

"Home," I thought, "I want to go home." I wanted to call out, but she was taking hold of my hands and helping me up from the floor.

"You must stand."

My legs wobbled. I felt unsteady and leaned against her, concentrating on taking a step, forgetting for the moment any more thoughts of family.

We moved on slowly, step by step, toward the opening at the front of her dwelling. "You must move, walk, become strong," she was saying. "Tomorrow we will go outside. The forest air is fresh. With time this too will help you heal."

"Tomorrow," I thought. "Something new is going to happen, then. I will become stronger—heal—but, for now, I must accept what has happened. I must remain here, at this place."

The morning air was cool, the sun just beginning to rise. I could see its misty beams spreading among the trees. A soft breeze blew through the tops of pines. Everything was bright green, hung with the sparkle of morning dew. The ground was damp and full of rich smells. Young seedlings had begun to take root on decaying trees that lay on the forest floor.

A pony was free-grazing in an open space a short distance from the dwelling, her coat the color of wheat. A streak of white ran across her withers and throughout her full mane and tail. She tossed her head, ears forward, looked at me, then went back to nibbling the sweet grass. After a time she raised her head again, sniffed the sharp clean air, and moved slowly into the dense pines. I noticed a large white splotch on her flank. It was in the shape of a butterfly.

"She is beautiful," I said.

"Her name is Kamali. It means Spirit Guide," Sewana replied. "She is going now to a stream to drink. Once she is finished, she will not stay alone in the woods but will return here. Sit now. In a while, walk about if you wish. Until you are fully healed, it is too early to wander far."

"I can't go anywhere even if I wanted to," I thought. "I'm dependent on this woman for everything. How can I go forward with my life?"

She walked into the hut and came out shouldering a woven bag. "When the sun is high, I will return," she said and headed toward the woods.

I sat, leaned against the dwelling, and began to study my surroundings again.

The hut was sturdy, an intricate entanglement of tree limbs with a long, tall lean-to braced against the outside. Not thirty feet away from me was a hammock made from stripped tree branches, smoothed, weathered to a soft grey, held securely by large limbs.

Flat-bottomed baskets made of boughs hung in the trees, each holding a strange plant. Within my reach, a ground dwelling of leaves and thinner boughs housed four lively hens and several rabbits. A goat, tethered to a stake with a long rope, munched grass nearby.

All this was strange to me, so unlike what I could remember of my family's home in Streeter. My eyes and ears studied the details surrounding me from the sounds to the dense woods to the blue sky above until at last I fell asleep.

Sewana was standing beside me when I awoke. I judged it to be about noon since the sun was directly overhead. She helped me to stand then led me inside. She laid the woven bag against a wall. Though I had not exerted myself that morning, my stomach was churning and I needed to eat.

After tending the cooking fire, she quickly heated the meal—broth again with leaves and meat. I downed two bowls then stretched out on my bed to rest.

That day she filled pottery jars with water from the nearby stream, brought them back, and heated them over the fire. Washing with that warmed water and getting rid of the dust and sweat made me feel like a new man.

As the days passed, I napped less and at night slept more soundly. My cough was almost gone. My eyes had lost their crustiness and were beginning to fully heal, their vision clearing, the lids returning to normal.

Later in the week when I was finally able to walk farther from the hut, I bathed in the stream where Kamali had gone to drink. The first time was a shock, the water freezing. It had come from up in the mountains... high country melted snow.

Sewana had told me to scrub my hair with my hands and my body with moss then rinse well. At first I wanted to climb back on the bank, I was so cold. But after a while I got used to it though my skin was always a bright pink after being in that water.

Soon enough, I felt better, well enough to leave the hut each morning but still too weak to wander far. It had been warm outside, the sky blue with idle clouds moving above the trees. A slight breeze rustled aspen leaves and pine needles gave off their sweet smell. Most of my time was spent leaning against a stump, thinking of my family in Streeter, wondering about Sewana, and watching the hens bother each other as they wandered about their enclosure.

Early each morning, Sewana left to gather healing herbs and edible plants. She knew those that could be eaten raw, those that must be cooked, those that were safe, and those that could be poisonous. I wondered how she had learned so much and vowed to ask her one day.

She brought back tufts of pine needles, showed me how to make a toothbrush and give my teeth a good scrubbing. "You will learn which pines are safe," she said. "Only chew their needles. Your mouth will feel fresh."

Often she'd bring back meat, mostly small game she had caught in a snare. Though I never saw her with a fishing pole, we did have fish now and then. And while I was still not able to go with her, she always shared her great knowledge of the forest with me.

LATE SPRING 1904

ARLY ONE MORNING I awoke to find Sewana moving about the room, rich smells coming from a skillet. Daylight was pinpointing its way through the door. I dressed and had just begun to eat my meal when she handed me a cloth sack.

"It is time to show you my forest," she said. "Today you come with me to gather."

I had a sudden feeling of excitement. Finally, I could go with her into the woods. With my desire to go, sad thoughts of my family and fear of "Ned" finding me were put aside for the time being. She extinguished the fire and wiped out the skillet. I watched as she slid a knife into a sheath at her waist then picked up two cloth bags. Filling one with some type of tools and leaving the other empty, she slung both over her shoulders.

I took the bag she had given me and followed her out of the hut. At first we moved quickly, leaving me slightly breathless. Farther into the woods we slowed, Sewana stepping more like a deer, carefully, silently. This was my first lesson in tracking.

"We have come early for a reason. Because of the morning dew, the leaves on the forest floor are soft and twigs do not snap under your feet. Where there are leaves, put each foot down slowly, gently, each step pushing forward. Listen to the sounds of the forest, the birds, the wind. Walk with these. Their noise will hide your steps."

The forest sounds came alive to me, then. Before that I had never thought about a bird's song, rustling trees, or the wind as something that would disguise my movements and stop a wild animal from knowing we were near.

"Watch for bare patches of earth. Pick your way where leaves and sticks are not thick. Notice trails where animals have been."

It was a lesson in how to move through the woods without disturbing its creatures—a lesson in how to hunt, how to survive.

We were on the edge of a meadow surrounded by deep woods when Sewana stopped and set her cloth sacks on the ground. The day was still cool, but the morning sun had begun to warm the area. A flutter of white butterflies moved lightly among the soft wild grasses and plants. The continuous hum of bees could be heard. Dandelions colored the open space. The smell of fresh earth was everywhere.

She had taken her herb tools from a sack and begun walking around the edge of the meadow. Streams of white butterflies seemed to be drawn to her, landing unafraid on her arms and shoulders. I watched as she bent then cut sections of certain plants and pulled at several roots, never taking more than a small amount of each. These she carefully bundled together and placed in the empty sack.

She spoke as she gathered. "Each time we may take what the Earth gives us. Take only what we will need. Let the rest remain. We will leave a token in return, a thank you to Mother Earth for her gifts." She reached into her sack, removed a pure white feather, and laid it gently on the ground.

"Now the sun is high and it is warm. Later trees will color and drop their leaves. Then we will have collected enough plants to feed us when snow falls. When winter leaves, new plants will reach up again and we will gather those. You will learn to gather and hunt by my side, to never eat anything unless you know what it is. Be patient. Listen and learn."

She continued moving through and around the meadow, choosing, bending, cutting, adding to her sack until the sun shone directly overhead.

"Now we go," she said quietly.

Each of our sacks was filled with cuttings or tools, and we carried bundles of plants in our arms. There were dandelion greens for salad, peppermint leaves for tea, wild berries, and many herbs.

"We have been given food for our table and healing herbs for when we need them," she said.

When we finally reached the hut, we set our bundles down inside and spilled the contents of our sacks on a ground cloth. Sewana showed me how to separate the plant leaves from the stems and spread them apart in single loose layers.

"Soon after they are found, the herbs must be dried. They are dry when they break in our hands. If they crumble, you have waited too long. Be patient. Loose plants and leafy herbs will dry first. Then the roots. When the time comes we will store them in clay jars and cover them with tight lids."

That day we worked until the afternoon light became pale and the cool night air seeped through the door. That night I slept as peacefully as I ever had, not even aware of the forest night noises.

Each day I became stronger. Many were spent in the same way, uncovering, naming, collecting, and drying plants until Sewana was confident I knew them well. Finally, I was able to go collect on my own. I had learned what I could and could not eat, what was poisonous and what was not. Sewana would check my find when I returned to the hut and found I never made a mistake. She would smile and I knew, then, that she was proud of my progress.

Even though I was alone at those times, my thoughts of running away had faded. I was still weak and had no idea of where I was.

A week later I was getting ready for a day spent in the meadow. Instead of our usual sacks, Sewana had slung one large woven bag over her back.

"Today we hunt. More teaching," she said, laughing at the huge smile on my face.

We began in the early morning. "Walk softly as you have been taught," she said. "Look for animal droppings and tracks. These will show the paths they travel."

It had been anther damp morning, so we were able to find our first tracks more easily. Sewana told me a rabbit had made them, and we began to follow the path of small prints. They led to a stream that worked its way through tall grasses, bent boughs, and tangled vines. There was an opening in the brush nearby.

"Here we will set our trap," she said.

She began by finding a broken branch and driving it into the ground then took two long, thin pieces of strong animal hide from her bag. One she tied in a loop, lowering and tightening it around the branch. The second she ran through the loop, stretching it up to the top of a bent bough near the stream.

"This is a snare," she explained, "a trap for rabbit, squirrel, raccoon, even possum. Always make more than one."

Handing me several thin pieces of the leather, she had me make three more snares. They weren't perfect, but I was willing to try.

"Now we must hide our tracks. No broken branch or bent grass should show that we were here. Spread mud from the stream. Throw pine needles around to hide our scent."

The morning after, we returned to the spot we had prepared to check our snares. Sure enough, we had caught a rabbit—one in her snare, none in mine.

Hunting for meat was not easy. Until I could make a proper snare, I would never catch an animal. But after a lot of failed tries, at long last I put together suitable snares and was rewarded with three rabbits. With Sewana's help, I skinned and cooked them, and that night I tasted the best meat I had ever had.

A few days later, Sewana decided it was time for me to trap something of size—a beaver. This time I shouldered the woven bag. She had placed the herb tools in her belt alongside the hunting knife. In her arms she carried an old steel trap. We followed the stream beyond our dwelling for quite a while until it spilled into a pond surrounded by stumps and branches of small, gnawed trees.

"See the teeth marks?" Sewana pointed. "Those were made by a beaver."

Nearby I saw a helter-skelter pile of sticks, logs, and mud poking above the water in rustic dome shapes. A ridge of branches stretched in a line alongside.

"That's a beaver dam and lodge. The dam stores their food and is for protection. The lodge is like a home for them."

I was continually amazed at her knowledge of the plants and animals around us. She always explained things so clearly. I mostly never asked questions about what we found but would instead just observe and listen.

"Under water are entrances where the beaver can move in and out," she continued. "Swim to the beaver dam. Push this into the mud where they have made an entrance to their lodge."

She handed me the trap.

I removed my clothes—all but my trousers. The trap couldn't have weighed more than five pounds, but once I was in the water, my body and pants wet, it seemed impossibly heavy. I wanted to let it go and swim back to shore, not be dragged down to the bottom of the pond. But I pushed myself forward instead, mumbling, "Just a little bit farther," over and over again.

Near the dam, the pond was actually shallow enough that my feet touched the bottom. Clutching the trap, I stood as tall as I could and looked back toward where I could see Sewana.

With hands cupped to her mouth she was shouting, "Push the trap down into the water and mud. Rub mud on the dam's tree limbs and sticks. That will hide your scent. We want the beaver to be forced to go one way into the dam. Find sticks floating in the water. At the place he will enter, make a kind of tunnel with them. He will go along that."

It seemed to take forever to scoop globs of mud from the shallow pond bottom, push it against the dam, and rub it on the limbs. Creating a tunnel through the dam and toward the lodge was another challenge. Grime and mud stuck in my hair and streaked my face. I was cold and miserable.

It was a much easier trek back to shore once I was free of the trap. "That was really a messy business," I protested as I climbed out, shook my body, and sat on the ground to catch my breath.

The following day we returned to check the trap. I carried a tool sack, Sewana a large skin bag I had not seen before.

Leaving my shirt and shoes behind, once again I sloshed into the water. From the sack Sewana had taken a long rope and held onto one end while I swam toward the lodge with the other. When I reached the dam, I could see clearly that the animal had been caught and was no longer alive.

"Attach your end of the rope to the trap and I will pull it to shore," she shouted.

Immediately after I swam back to Sewana, she released the dead beaver from the trap, removed the hide, and finally cut the meat into small pieces. I was told to line the skin bag with moss from the lake, which would absorb liquid from the meat as we carried it home.

It had been a full day and, at the moment, all I could think about was heading for the hut, eating a good meal, and resting. I lifted the bag of beaver meat to my shoulder. Sewana carried the trap and tool sack.

At first I didn't really think it was worth going through all that trouble just to trap a beaver. But I realized soon enough that when winter came, we would need its warm pelt for clothing and smoked meat to keep us fed.

It had taken time to prepare the pelt and smoke the meat, and the herbs we had dried also needed to be stored in jars, so it was several days before we went to the woods again.

The morning we left for a high mountain meadow, one I had not yet seen, we took a different trail than we usually did. Sewana wanted to show me ways of reaching other gathering spots and hunting grounds. The steep climb revealed that I still did not have my full strength as I needed to rest often. The time with "Ned" and my illness had taken their toll on me.

We spent the morning picking plants. Sewana taught me their names as we put them in the sacks we carried.

When the sun was high above the pines, we left for the hut, enjoying the warmth of the day and following the chatter of squirrels hidden in their high tree nests. After a mile or so, I needed to stop and rest again while Sewana gathered pine needles for our bedding.

Within minutes she came out from the edge of the woods, looked about cautiously, then signaled me to come. I stood and quietly walked over to her. There on the ground near a clump of bushes were scattered red droppings and a bloody pattern of prints. My heart raced.

Sewana bent down to study them. "Wolf," she whispered.

We moved forward, following the pattern. The woods became thicker, the air lighter, and within a short while we lost sight of the droplets. There was silence in the forest. No movement from a single creature, no breeze in the high pines.

Then, unexpectedly the blood trail reappeared, the drops closer together, at times a shallow red puddle here and there. "The wolf must be in agony," I thought, though we heard nothing, not a whimper.

"It has probably run a long way to escape something or someone," I said softly. "I would have thought it would have collapsed by now..."

Before I had finished my sentence, there was the wolf, blocking our path, lying by the banks of a creek. It was smaller than I might have guessed, its grey coat matted with blood. It had vomited.

Sewana stood still for a moment then moved forward to kneel beside the wounded animal. Cautiously she reached out and began to stroke the hairs on its back, moving in one soothing motion from neck to tail, all the while speaking in gentle tones. The wolf didn't stir.

"She-Wolf," she said as I moved closer.

Pressing her hands lightly along the weakened body, she searched for the wound. With that the animal began to whimper, its legs twitching, its stomach straining. Then within seconds, the wolf's tail lifted. A round form emerged... a pup wrapped in its birth sac.

On our farm in Streeter, I had watched my dog deliver a litter of five puppies in a corner of our tool shed. She was a healthy mutt who took over the delivery without any help from me. She'd strain a bit then lift her tail and push a pup out wrapped in a thin, see-through skin. With her tongue she'd lick this open, lap it up, then bite through the umbilical cord that connected her to her pup. There was a lot of time between births, so she was able to clean each pup before the next one came along.

But this wolf did not have the strength to care for her newborn. It was up to us.

As soon as the pup had shown, Sewana quickly lifted it and gently removed the transparent skin. She took a thin string of sinew from her woven bag, tied it tightly around the cord, cut the separation with her knife, then brought the animal's tiny face to hers and blew into its mouth and nose.

No response.

I watched with fascination as she cupped it carefully and firmly in her hands, then swung it in her arms between her legs a few times. Raising it to her mouth, she blew again. When its little body began to squirm ever so slightly, she handed it to me.

"Empty your herb bag. Use it to rub this little one carefully, quickly. Keep it breathing," she said. "Another will be born soon."

I emptied my bag, laid it on the ground, took the pup from Sewana, and rubbed as I'd been told. There was a soft squeal from the tiny mouth, and I felt an incredible thrill as it responded to the massage.

Sewana was working on the second pup that had appeared, cleaning, massaging, blowing, swinging—all the moves I had seen her do with the first to start the breathing. At times she would listen to its chest, checking for a heartbeat.

"Rub," she said, finally holding out the second pup to me.

I laid it next to the first and began to massage both of them at once. While I worked with the two pups, Sewana kneeled next to the she-wolf anticipating the birth of a third, but nothing seemed to be happening.

"They take time to birth," she said. "Sometimes hours."

Her hands moved across the wolf's head, along the back, around the belly, stopping at the area where the heart would be. She lowered her head against that spot to listen then pushed on the belly with both hands.

No movement. The wolf lay perfectly still.

"She is gone," Sewana said after several minutes. Yet she kept pressing her hands over and around the wolf's stomach then putting her ear to its heart. It was as if she wanted the animal to come alive again.

Then, "Wait," she said, lifting her head and staring at me. "There are more. They will not come on their own now."

She rolled the dead wolf onto its back. The herb knife was in her hand, and she began cutting from the middle of the chest down to the bottom of the belly. Within seconds she had folded back the thick skin, reached between the flaps, and was lifting out a long slippery tube-like section. Carefully, she cut this open and removed two more pups.

Handing me one, we both began the same procedure as we had on the first two. But neither animal responded. We worked feverishly at the same time, continuing to massage the pups that had been born earlier.

Finally, Sewana laid her newborn next to the she-wolf. "No use," she said. "Too much of the mother's blood lost while they were still inside her. You must stop now too. Lay your pup near the other."

I heard her but could not stop breathing into my pup's nose and mouth. Tears ran down my face. Sewana was watching me, knowing that I was unable to give up. Then I heard a tiny whimper, ever so faint it was a wonder that I had not missed it.

"He's alive," I whispered as the body began to squirm and make a squealing noise. I placed the bundle next to the other two.

That moment I felt a deep connection to the newborn pups. At the dugout in Ruff, I too had struggled to survive, but a kind person had saved me. I was alive, learning to live a new life, one that I had never known or even imagined.

"Keep them together for warmth," Sewana was saying, "and keep massaging them."

I hoped she would help me, but instead she walked away. She neared a clearing not far from where we were and pulled at sections of grass until a wide opening had been cleared and the ground was visible. I watched from where I sat with the pups.

She reached for her root tool and started to dig. The dirt was loose, so she would scoop with her hands then use the tool until she had a fairly substantial hole.

"Now you will dig," she said, handing me the root tool and taking my place beside the pups. It was tiring work, but finally the hole was deep and long enough to hold the body of the she-wolf and her pup.

I took over care of the other pups while Sewana gathered tufts of soft grass. With these she lined the hole, pressing it into the sides and bottom.

Going over to the she-wolf, she pushed the rounded tube that had held the pups back into its body. Then taking a thin strip of hide and a bone needle from her bag, she sewed the incision she had made earlier until it was neatly closed.

While I watched, she emptied the herbs from her sack and dipped it into the cool water of the creek nearby. Kneeling next to the wolf, she began cleaning the matted blood from its coat until its fur seemed to shine more silver than grey. Then together we lifted the body, carried it to the grave and lowered it onto the blanket of grass.

I was back with the pups when Sewana went to the stream again. She rinsed her bloodied sack then returned to the dead pup. It was so small that she could hold the tiny body with one hand while washing it with the cloth in her other hand. Carrying it to the grave, she gently lay the still body by its mother's belly.

Bunches of loose grass still lay on the ground. Sewana placed layer after layer atop and around the two bodies until they were covered then slowly crumbled loosened dirt atop the grass blanket. All the while I marveled at the care and respect she showed these wild creatures.

When the hole was completely covered, she began to search for rocks. Finding some of substantial size, she asked me to carry them to the grave where we stacked one after another. "So wild animals will not dig up this spot," she said.

I sat by the pups while Sewana stood quietly beside the grave. Her eyes were closed, her arms raised above her head. She began swaying from side to side. Within a few moments she uttered a chord over and over, no words, no real melody. Then, in a soft, sing-song voice, she began to chant:

"Earth mother,

Honor my sister the She-Wolf.

Take her pup,

Hold him

Against your heart."

Sewana knelt beside the grave, placed her hands upon the rocks, swayed side to side, and continued chanting. I was transfixed, never having seen anything like this before.

When the ritual had finished, she stood and turned to me. "Wrap the wolf pups in your shirt," she said. "We will take them to the hut."

We began down the trail again, Sewana behind me shouldering the woven sacks. My thoughts were on the bundle in my arms and how we now had three newborn wolves to care for. I couldn't help but smile.

About halfway to the hut, I came around a bend. Before we would reach the next stand of pine, the path ahead was mostly weeds and brush with a few large berry bushes crowding out whatever else might grow there.

Holding the pups against me with one arm, I reached out to see if any berries had ripened, remembering their sweet juice and how the first of the season always seemed to be the most delicious. A low whimper startled me.

I turned to Sewana. "Over here," I whispered and pointed toward the sound.

She moved to the tangled shrubs and stopped to listen. All was quiet at first, then, after a minute or so, there was an unmistakable moan. Sewana separated the lower branches, looked within, then motioned for me to come closer. A few yards from us, under a hollow of curved dry plant stems, a grown wolf lay on its side. Blood pooled around his hind legs and matted his tail.

"A male," she said.

She bent over and with great care patted its head, running her hands down its large body to search for a wound. "Both the she-wolf and this one have been attacked by a bear," she told me. "Their wounds were from a big animal, not from trap or gun. Her cubs were in danger. The mother bear was defending her own."

"Could this day become any stranger?" I wondered.

"The wolf's breath comes slowly. We must take him with us to the hut or he too will die."

"Impossible," I thought as she spoke—she with her tools and herb sacks, me with the pups. How could we possibly manage?

Without another word, Sewana walked ahead to where the heavy forest began again, then reappeared dragging two sturdy greyed branches. In length they seemed to be about my height. She laid them out on the ground in the shape of a triangle, wide end at the bottom, narrow at the top.

Taking her knife from its sheath, she sliced open our two empty herb sacks, then quickly sewed them together with a strip of sinew. This one single piece of strong wide fabric could now be secured over the two poles, creating a platform at the bottom of the wider base.

"Give me your shirt," she said.

I unwound the pups and held them close to my chest for warmth then handed her my shirt. Stretching it out, she slipped each sleeve over the poles at the narrower top then twisted and tied the remaining material around the branches at the bottom. She dragged the finished frame close to the bushes.

"Set the pups down gently. Help me move the wolf from the hollow."

I set the three down and walked the few steps with Sewana into the bushes. The wolf had stopped whimpering, lay eerily quiet, his breaths coming in shallow spurts. It took several minutes for us to lift him out, for the animal was heavy.

Carefully, we rolled him onto the cloth platform. He didn't move or make a sound.

"It is a long way to the hut," Sewana said. "We will take turns carrying the pups and pulling the platform. That will make the walk easier."

She picked up the poles at the top, one in each hand and held them waist high. For such a slight woman, her arms seemed strong as she began moving forward, down the trail, dragging the frame behind her. The wolf lay motionless. I gathered up the pups and followed.

When she tired, we traded jobs. I could feel the weight of the poles on my hands and in my arms. The frame was more easily pulled along the downward trail, more difficult to move through the shrubs. The heaviest part of the wolf's body was balanced in the center. This proved to make the entire frame easier to drag, and sharing the effort made it less tiring.

We walked along quietly. The distance seemed far yet not overwhelming since our minds were focused on caring for the animals we had rescued.

We arrived at the hut as the sun was dipping low in the pines. My arms ached from dragging the frame, but I didn't complain for Sewana never said a word about how tired she must have been. She went to the hut, brought out a worn blanket, and laid it next to the base of the frame. "Lift him onto this," she said.

Together we slid the wolf onto the blanket.

"I will take care of him out here," she said. "You care for the pups inside."

At first she followed me into the hut. I was relieved since I had no idea what to do.

"Long days are ahead of us," Sewana said. "Days and nights of feeding and caring. We will act as their mother."

She moved about the hut, taking a blanket from a shelf, arranging it on the ground in a circle, and rolling the sides into a thick protective wall. Then she gently took each of the pups from me and set them on the blanket. The three pups snuggled together, one on top of the other, their little noses barely poking out from under each other's round bellies.

"They will stay warm in here," she said. "Keep them together. Massage them. When I am finished with the wolf, I will come inside to help you. They must eat soon."

I wondered how we would feed them since the she-wolf was no longer with us.

Several covered pots sat on the floor around the room. Sewana carried two of them to the outside of the hut then returned to pick up a cloth bag, a basket of rags, and an empty jug. She reached for an Indian peace pipe that hung on the wall and handed it to me. "While I am outside, twist off its bowl. I will milk the goat as soon as I can, and we will use the clay pipe stem like a baby bottle to feed the pups."

The pipe was sturdy, the stem formed of red clay, rounded and polished to a fine sheen. The bowl was the stub of an antler. I twisted the antler this way and that, trying to dislodge the bowl. At first I was gentle, afraid of cracking the pipe stem, but after a time, frustrated that it wasn't coming loose, I gave the antler a sharp bang on the ground. There was a faint "pop."

Thinking I might have damaged the pipe stem, I looked it over carefully. Not a crack. But the bowl had loosened and when I twisted this time, it came off in my hands. I blew through the pipe stem, and it made a sharp whistling sound.

After checking the pups, now fast asleep on top of each other, I went outside. Sewana was working on the wounded wolf. A pot of water and some rags were sitting by his side. Though he still hadn't moved from where we had laid him on the blanket, I could see that he was breathing.

"How are the pups?" Sewana asked.

"Asleep. Snuggled together in a tight little pile."

Several rags from the basket were soaked with water and lay on the ground. They must have been used to clean the blood and dirt from the deep wound located on the wolf's right hind leg.

"It was important to stop the bleeding. The wound must be clean before I treat it with herbs," she said as she poured the last of the water over the opening.

When she lifted the lid on one of the pots, I saw that it contained honey. She poured a small amount into the wound. "To keep the infection away," she said simply as I watched.

She untied the knot on a cloth bag. "Moss. This I have squeezed dry and pressed flat into pieces. All dirt and twigs are gone. It stays clean in this bag."

She reached within and slowly slid out a large green square, then pressed it to the wound. The wolf's eyes stayed closed. He never moved or made a sound.

"Now the pups," Sewana said as she stood and walked toward the lean-to. "I'll milk the goat and bring the milk inside."

I went back to the pups, and, shortly after, she returned to the hut carrying the jug filled with goat's milk. She pulled a fresh egg from her pocket and added its yolk to the liquid. A small piece of cotton rag had been sitting near the fire pit. Sewana poured some milk onto the rag then told me to pick up one of the pups.

From the two males and one female, I chose the one that I had brought back to life, the smallest of the three, a little male. He nestled down in my arms. Sewana handed me the wet rag and had me hold it to his mouth. He squealed, and when he did, opened his mouth just wide enough for me to put the rag against it. Then he began to suck, the milky liquid oozing down his chin.

Next she covered one end of the peace pipe stem with animal skin, tightening it in place with sinew. Pouring milk into the other end, she pressed a small square of transparent skin over the tip, securing it too with sinew. Into this she poked a tiny hole.

"Sit on your blanket. Lean the pup against your body and hold his head up. Press the tip against his mouth so he can taste a drop of milk."

At first he squirmed, but, soon finding he was in for a treat, began to suck. For probably two whole minutes he drank, and then fell asleep in my arms.

"Now burp him," Sewana said. "Put him over your shoulder and rub his back."

I laid my cheek alongside his head and patted his back.

"You're not finished yet," she said and handed me a warm wet rag. "Every time any of them eat, you gently rub this on their bottom. It will help them wet. After, you must bathe them."

I had to handle each pup the same way. By the time all three were safely back in their bed, their tummies full, I was exhausted. Sewana left the hut again to care for the grown wolf. She called to me that nothing had changed. He had not yet moved and seemed to be in a deep sleep.

That night we went without much rest. All three pups had to be fed several times and ate as though they were starving. It was clean the pipe stem, collect the milk, feed and clean their little bodies over and over. I slept when they slept, only waking when one of them cried out. Every time I'd tend to the pups inside Sewana had to attend to the injured wolf outside.

Two days and nights passed before the older wolf became conscious. His eyes opened and with great difficulty he struggled to stand. Sewana called me from the hut to watch.

His eyes stayed fixed on hers. Whether daring her to move or not, I wasn't certain. She stood perfectly still as he came toward her step by agonizing step, his injured leg dragging along the ground. When he finally reached her, he laid his head against her side.

For a few minutes she did not move then, carefully lowering one hand, put it under the animal's muzzle. He sniffed it several times then licked her palm. Slowly she reached up and gently rubbed him behind the ears and along his back. From that moment on the wolf was allowed into the hut with us. Sewana thought it would be good for the pups to be near him. At night he slept by their bed as if to guard them.

His wound was treated each evening. Sewana named him "Strong One," and he learned to come whenever she called.

While I cared for the pups during the day, Sewana continued searching for herbs, trapping on her own, taking care of the caged animals, and cooking. The grown wolf stayed by her side and showed remarkable skill as he learned how to move about quickly using only his three legs. He would probably never put weight on the injured leg again.

Eventually, things let up a little. The pups were growing fast. We had begun to let them taste mushy meat off our fingers before giving them the bottle.

As they grew stronger and we were certain they would survive, Sewana asked me to name them. The girl I called "Minya," the Indian name for "older sister." Since she was the first born, the name fit. The second born, a male, we called "Wahya" or "wolf," the third "Minsun" or "little brother."

By now their eyes had fully opened and to my surprise were a light blue. The three would explore the blanket, working their way over the edge. "Strong One" was always there to carry them back if they moved toward the hut's open door.

Sewana took responsibility for the grown wolf while my life revolved around the three pups. She warned me not to let them think they were ever in charge. From the beginning they must learn I was the great wolf of the pack. I felt my courage had become stronger and stronger since I had escaped "Ned" and arrived in the forest with

Sewana. Now I was strong enough to lead my wolves. Be their teacher. Their Alpha.

So, at about the time they started eating meat and lapping water from a bowl the real training began. Because I had grown to love them, disciplining the three would not be easy. I'd held them, played with them, let them fall asleep next to me on my bedding. Now I faced the challenge of moving away from these things somewhat and I found that worrisome. Could I be kind and still be firm?

The training began with their food. I'd eat first then fill their bowls with warm goat's milk mixed with bits of animal meat. They'd sniff at the liquid then poke their mouths into it, coming up with droplets on their muzzles. I could almost hear them thinking, "No more bottle" as three pink tongues began to lap.

The many lessons went on: "Always have them walk behind you, eat after you. Do not use a lot of words. Speak with a strong voice, gentle hands, arms, eyes, and mouth. Never show weakness or they will challenge you. Never strike them. Do all with kindness. Then they will follow you." These were Sewana's words.

SUMMER AND FALL 1904

ND SO BEGAN THEIR growth out of pup-hood. From the lapping bowl we went on to fill bowls with only meat, sometimes adding animal bones, fur, and feathers. We had to trap mice and now and then sacrifice a chicken for them.

"In the wild they will have to hunt, feed themselves. Someday you will not be there to feed them," Sewana explained. "What we are giving them now is like what they will hunt and eat, then."

I kept up with the training as Sewana had told me to do. I'd take the pups outside and let them play in front of the hut. They'd pick up leaves and twigs and strut around with them in their mouths as if they had found a treasure. They were curious about stones, feathers, and bits of fur we placed on the ground. They'd paw and bite at them then, tiring of the game, turn on each other, nipping, squealing, and rolling about until they would drop down exhausted. Sometimes it was difficult to use a stern voice if they misbehaved. "They're just pups," I thought. But in my heart I knew they had to learn discipline.

Then came the day when they could venture farther. They knew my signal—a sharp whistle—and would come running, circle around my legs, and nip at my pants for attention. There was never a rope around their necks, nothing to keep them from leaving. And, in a short while, because I had taught them well, they learned to trot along beside me when I called.

At first we didn't wander far from home. The pups jumped from one bush to another, sniffing and making their mark. They were fascinated by the bees sucking nectar from the wild flowers and stuck their noses in so close that I was afraid they might get stung. But at my command, they always left what they were doing and returned to me.

The day of "pounce training" (or "how to catch your own dinner"), we arrived home after one of our outings as the sun came over the top of the pines. There was a patch of ground alongside the hut near some heavy bunches of sweet grass. There we would begin.

I began the new game by tying a small square of fur to a long string of sinew. The pups were tumbling about, wiggling and scratching their backs against the ground. I placed the fur near them and walked to the sweet grass, the sinew in my hand. I stood there quietly watching them for a while then gave a quick sudden jerk on the string.

The fur popped up like it was alive. All three stopped scratching and turned their heads toward the action. I jiggled the string again. The pups turned, eyes, ears, and noses pointed at the target. They walked closer to the fur then stopped, stared, heads lowered, eyes alert.

At that moment, I pulled the sinew toward me. As one, all three ran toward the fur, leapt in the air, and landed on the "prey," trying to grab it in their front paws. There was a scramble for who would be the one to keep the prize. It was Wahya. Minya and Minsun moved to one side, letting Wahya be the first to claim the "kill." After nipping at it for a while, he backed away, allowing the other two to inspect.

Strong One lay on a grassy patch beside the hut watching the three. He seemed to be thinking, "I already know all about this kind of thing, but the pups have a lot to learn."

We trained like this every day even in the rain. They were growing fast and had to be taught what their mother would have taught them had she lived. They needed to survive in the wild on their own. For one day, when we set them free, I couldn't help thinking of the dangers, predators they would face, and perhaps men like "Ned."

While I trained the pups, Sewana would be gone from the hut for hours, Strong One at her side. She'd return with sacks of herbs and roots and explain their uses to me. There were camas roots, wild potatoes, and carrots. There were wild onions, mint, and dandelion. Although she had once hunted with a bow, it was now difficult for her to bring back a deer alone, so she mostly used snares to catch rabbit, squirrel, and birds. Then one day she said, "Tomorrow we shall go for herbs and roots together. The pups are ready to come along."

I hoped she would be pleasantly surprised at how well they followed orders and how they kept close to me. It had been hard for me to stay back while I was training the pups and not wander in the forest with her. The pups could sense that something new was about to take place. While Strong One watched, they ran around the hut stumbling over one another, nipping each other's mouths.

All of us left the hut together. The sun was warm, the earth beneath us soft, the ground leaves crunching under feet and paws. Tall grasses bent as we walked through them. The pups bounded around my legs at first, staying close, excited about being away from the hut. The farther we walked, the more we had to stop while they sniffed out new surroundings, poked at bugs, stuck their muzzles into rotting logs, and left their mark every twelve feet or so.

"Minya, Wahya, Minsun," I'd call then whistle. Their heads would lift, their ears perk up, a curious look would fill their eyes. I was becoming impatient, wanting to hurry them along.

"Let them be," Sewana said. "They are marking their territory, getting used to things. Finding their way."

It occurred to me then that Sewana's real purpose for this trip was not to gather herbs and plants but rather to have the pups learn more about what was farther from the hut. "They will be on their own someday," had been her words. Tears filled my eyes at the thought. I knew in my heart she was right. And I knew that I would be on my own someday as well, moving away from Sewana's world back into the one I had once known before my westward journey.

With the pups tagging along, it probably took us three times longer to arrive at the meadow than it had when Sewana and I had gone there in the past. At first they jumped around through the tall grass, weeds and flowers, nosing at bees and butterflies, batting at each other, knocking one another over, and running as fast as they might in what appeared to be a game of wolf-tag.

Finally, they tired, grouped together, and lay down where the meadow edged the woods. The pups lay quiet while we dug and clipped, putting as many plants as we could in a woven bag and bundling several so that we might easily carry them. While we worked, small white butterflies began to gather, the light from the sun reflecting off their delicate wings as they danced about the meadow flowers. They seemed to be everywhere, landing on blossoms then closing their wings, opening them again, and swiftly swirling quietly into the sky above.

"Cabbage butterflies," Sewana called to me. "They like the mustard plants."

They flew around her noiselessly, landing on her head and shoulders. They were whiter than snow. A tiny black spot dabbed their forewings and a bit of yellow traced along both back wings. Not one came to me, even when I stood perfectly still. They seemed only drawn to her and would not leave even when she moved or bent to choose another plant.

The sun was high when Sewana put the bag over her shoulder. I collected the bundles and whistled for Minya, Wahya, and Minsun. They came trotting over, but when Sewana and I began to walk, the three no longer hugged my legs. Instead, they took off, running ahead, and no amount of my calling or whistling brought them back. I noticed that Strong One followed after them.

"They head for home, wanting to eat. They know the way now," Sewana said.

Her saying that did not comfort me. What if they got lost? Sewana didn't seem at all concerned.

It took us a while to arrive at the hut. All four were already inside, curled up by their bowls. They pestered me until I set their food in front of them.

"Soon the young ones must learn to hunt on their own for when they are grown they must leave," Sewana said.

"They can stay..." I said, "be with me. I'll care for them. Take them home with me when I go from here."

"It cannot be. Their spirit is one with nature. They must be free to roam, live their lives among their own as you are meant to live among your own," she said.

"But I have raised them," I protested. "They know me. They love me."

"Then you must let them go."

I knew then that she was also speaking of me. I would need to leave this place one day and return to my own family and home where I was meant to be. But my heart was torn between these two places, the farm I had left behind in Streeter and this mountain heaven which I loved.

The fall weather was becoming cooler, the days shorter. While the pines would stay green, the other trees had brilliant leaves of yellow, red, and bronze. On some early mornings dew cold be found frozen on the ground leaves. It was clear there was no more waiting. We must teach our wolves to hunt. They were equipped for the job: long legs for running, strong teeth and jaws for holding prey, and their natural instincts. And then one day a touch of snow fell, the feathered flurries tasting sweet on my tongue. My breath formed puffs of icy smoke in the air. We began serious training immediately.

"With winter coming soon, they must learn to hunt prey and no longer depend on us to feed them. We will need our stored food for our own use and do not know how long that supply will last," Sewana reminded me.

We started each training session at dusk, the time when they would usually search for prey. Sewana had taken a rabbit carcass, touched it to the ground here and there, making a trail-scent that would lead to the stream near the meadow. There she buried the dead animal in a shallow hole. Hopefully, Minya, Wahya, and Minsun would follow the scent then dig where the animal lay.

As planned, we all started out together, Strong One as usual walking beside Sewana. The maturing pups soon caught the scent of the carcass and began to hurry along, running some, then slowing, noses almost to the ground. They seemed to work as a team. We lost sight of them at once.

By the time we approached the stream bank, they had already dug up the rabbit and had devoured it—meat, bones and fur—with their powerful jaws. There were no leftovers, and all three were sitting, licking their fur and grooming themselves.

That evening when we returned to the hut, Sewana had Strong One and the pups sleep outside for the first time. I objected but she said it was time for them to learn to be on their own.

"But what if they leave?" I complained.

"They will not leave yet," she replied.

I hardly slept that night and kept peeking out the hut door to see if they were still there. Though I was quiet, they always raised their heads and, seeing it was me, went back to sleep.

At twilight the next evening, we walked with them a short distance into the forest. It didn't take long before they left us, one trailing the other. This time Strong One followed.

"Look at the sky," Sewana said as she watched five ravens circle overhead, about a mile from us. "They will go there." She pointed to the trees below the birds.

We hurried to the site. The distance was less than we had expected. Not wanting to alert them, we approached downwind and hid among the undergrowth. They had not yet eaten but were lying near a dead raccoon. Its scent had drawn them to it.

Minya, the little girl, had lowered herself to the ground on one side of the animal while Minsun approached the prey from the other. Wahya, the largest of the three, nipped then tapped it with his paw. He began to tear off pieces of meat and, after a few minutes, allowed Minya, Minsun, and Strong One to feed.

Sewana and I watched for a while then silently backed among the trees and returned to the hut. Several hours later all four showed up, lay down outside curled about each other, and slept.

"They have the drive to hunt," Sewana said. "They will find the dead or weakened easily. Now they must learn to take down a live prey."

WINTER 1904-1905

T HE SNOWS WERE BEGINNING to come each day
with greater force, not yet piling up the side of
the hut but threatening.

I had cut some good-sized logs. These rotten stumps
and fallen branches were stacked outside the hut almost
to the top of its dome. At night the door was covered over
with several deer hides to keep out the chill.

When there was a partial or full moon, shadows
lengthened over the snow-covered ground. We often
heard the crackling of trees as ice caked them and wind
swayed the frozen branches.

There was a sudden hush over everything during the
day, while in the dark we often heard faint movements,
probably those of tiny night creatures searching for
something to eat. The wolves slept most of each day,
digging down in their own snow cave, warmed by each

other and the closeness of our hut. They had become secure in their hunts, finding raccoons, rabbits, mice, and an occasional squirrel. At dusk they would leave, returning later in the night. They never begged anything from us and always seemed to have eaten their fill. Yet, I was still concerned that they had not, to our knowledge, taken down a larger animal.

One morning I awoke to find the wolves gone. The ground where they had slept was covered with a dusting of fresh snow, their tracks invisible. I told Sewana I wanted to leave and look for them. She said I should stay, that they would be back, but I was worried. So, I dressed in warm clothing—hooded coat, pants, gloves, winter moccasins—and headed out into the cold morning air.

My breath came in pants at first as the shock of leaving the warm hut for the brisk out-of-doors hit me. I sucked in gulps of air then blew out streams of fog, watching it float away like a grounded cloud. The sun was shining through the pines, the fine dusting on the needles sifting like flour toward the forest floor.

After a while, the wolf tracks became more visible, the top layer of the snow having blown off. The remaining heart-shaped back pad, the toes and claws of each of their feet, had been placed firmly in the fallen crystals, forming an unmistakable print. They were walking in a single file, one behind the other. This time Strong One was leading, his crippled leg held high, his three paw prints visible.

Their path moved steadily forward. There was no indication of being in a hurry.

I continued to follow the trail while nibbling on some dried deer meat and hard-boiled eggs from my coat pocket and drinking melted snow from my gloved hands. The wind was slight, so the cold did not seem overpowering. But I knew I had to keep moving to stay warm.

The sun had risen over the treetops when I spotted a change of direction in the tracks. They had moved off the trail deeper into the forest. I watched the ground and saw that they had circled in and out among a grove of lodge-pole pine, weaving among the tall, thin trunks. Their paws had begun to crisscross each other, then mingle with a different track altogether. A deer!

Not small enough to belong to a fawn or large enough for a buck. I figured these prints belonged to a doe.

Farther along, the ground became a sprawling mass of both hoof and paw prints intertwined, matted one upon the other. The white ground cover had been churned up in whatever frenzied battle had taken place. Splashes of blood had fallen and formed frozen scarlet patterns against the white snow.

Then the cluster of tracks seemed to suddenly rush back to the trail again where I realized the chase had truly begun in earnest. The distance of the doe's hooves had become streamlined, a prey fleeing for its life. Wolf tracks flew forward, closing in, bounding through the snow in pursuit. I continued moving forward as quietly and quickly as I could.

Engrossed with the tracking, I suddenly realized I was far from the hut. I must have gone at least five miles through a part of the woods I had not seen before. About a quarter mile ahead I could see a barrier of rock so tall it would have taken a rope to climb. Moving steadily closer I stopped, knelt noiselessly in the snow, and stared at the spectacle before me.

Minya, Minsun, Wahya, and Strong One lay asleep on the ground at the rock base, their thick fur tails curved over their snouts, their bodies up against one another. Nearby was the carcass of a deer. Not much was left of the animal, just some muscle, bone, and the hide. After the chase, with instinctive precision, they had cornered their already injured prey against the rocky outcrop.

Silently I moved backward, happy that I was downwind, my human smell made indistinguishable. Though they had been trained by me, I wasn't certain how the wolves would have reacted to me surprising them while they slept next to their kill. The forest would hide me while I moved and followed the trail of animal prints back toward the hut and Sewana.

It happened when I was about three miles from the hut. After having begun as gentle flakes, out of nowhere the snow came with a vengeance, its blinding force so strong I knew I had to stop or run the risk of becoming lost. Though the animal prints would now be covered, I was certain I could still find my way home.

A shelter had to be constructed quickly. I had to keep myself warm and dry until the storm blew over. I thought of Sewana and wondered if she would be worried if I didn't return home that night. Fortunately, the woods were good to me. Barely off the trail was a tree, bent so that its trunk touched the ground, rooted firmly, then reached for the sky once more. I began by finding fallen branches half covered with snow strewn around the area. Tugging them from the ground, I quickly formed makeshift walls and a roof against the bent tree.

Finishing with the branches, I began digging out the snowdrift beneath its trunk, packing this against the outside of the shelter, making a protective shield. Where the snowdrift had once been I laid pine boughs over the depression. It was a small shelter but would stay warm since there was no excess space, and, fortunately, it also faced away from the wind.

I crawled inside, sat on the pine boughs, and watched through a small open section as the world outside turned into a complete whiteout. The wind was relentless, but the shelter held tight. Tired from the worry of following the wolves, overwhelmed by the sudden appearance of this monster storm, but thankful that I was safe and warm, I fell asleep.

At first it was a restless sleep including sounds of the wind, the cold around me, the wolves, but then I settled into a dream, this time of my home in Streeter, my mother and sister, my father. And deep down, I felt a deep sense of loneliness.

When I awoke, the noise from the wind had stopped. Rays of sun were gathering on the shelter floor and on the silver-grey hairs of a wolf curled up beside me.

Minya. When I moved she stood, shook herself, and moved out through a small opening she must have dug on one side of the shelter. When had she come? Where were the others?

I stood and shook out the kinks in my own body. I looked through the opening. The other three were standing there, a slight dusting of snow on their backs from having slept outside. They seemed to have been waiting for me to come out and walk the trail with them. I could almost read their thoughts, "Just another day in the wilderness... here we are... let's head home."

And homeward bound it was, though more of a difficult trek for me this time because of the night's storm. This didn't seem to bother the wolves since their paw pads and the webbing between each of their toes helped them move over the snow easily. But it seemed they respected the fact that I was trudging along through heavy drifts and held their pace to a slower walk. I no longer had to worry about how to find my way to the hut.

They led the way down the trail, which had now been concealed by the fallen snow. Though I sometimes slipped and fell on hidden ice, their blunt claws gripped any slippery surface and they stood strong. Their heavy coats had grown thick with the winter cold, keeping them dry and warm. I found I too was warm under my layers of homemade deerskin and cotton clothing.

We had started in the morning, yet it took a long while to reach the hut. By the time we had traveled the miles, night had settled in. The dark sky beamed with stars and a partial moon. They helped light our way, but the wolves, I was certain, would have found the hut in any case.

Somehow Sewana must have heard us coming. She was standing at the door, a glow from the fire pit seeping through the sides of the deerskin she held away from its opening. She had wrapped herself in an old buffalo hide. Only her head was visible. Not a hint of how she felt about us having been gone for almost two full days showed on her face.

"The storm came up suddenly when I was out looking for them," I said, pointing to the wolves.

All four stood, tails wagging, their muzzles seeming to smile. Meanwhile I kept talking, trying to explain my absence, filling in every detail of the tracking, the deer, the storm. When I had run out of words, Sewana turned back into the hut. I followed.

"We eat first. Then the animals," she said abruptly, then poured hot stew from a pan on the glowing fire into two bowls. She handed one to me.

"Good thing I had dried beef and hard eggs with me, or I think I might have starved," I said.

"I had told you not to go," she said not looking at me. "They would have returned on their own. The storm might have taken you. They can take care of themselves." After that, she was silent.

I swallowed a full bowl of the meat and vegetables, wiping the juice from the bottom of the bowl with warm bread Sewana had made. "How did you make this?" I asked, hoping to break the silence. "I've never tasted anything so good."

Sewana rolled her eyes. For a while she didn't answer. Then, like my grandmother who shared her recipes with anyone who seemed to enjoy her cooking, decided with a shrug to tell me.

"The nuts and seeds we both gathered. The grains were stored on the shelves. I ground them with a stone until they became powder, mixed that with goat's milk, flattened it with my hands, then baked it."

She paused. "I worried when you were gone so long," she said, finally looking at me.

After the meal, both of us cleaned the bowls with heated water. It was time to feed the wolves.

Outside the hut I set dried meat in front of the wolves, who were almost asleep in the snow. For the first time since they had been born, they didn't seem at all interested in their food, rising just enough to sniff it.

I drew the door hide aside. "They aren't eating," I called out. "They haven't even touched the food."

"Because of the deer," Sewana said. "They ate their fill. In a few days they will eat again. Bring the meat inside. We will save it for later."

I re-entered the hut, set the meat aside, and peeked out the doorway again. Minya, Wahya, Minsun, and Strong One were asleep, their warm furry coats touching, their bodies dug down in the snow. I stepped back, then sat by the slow-burning fire in the center of the room, its thin smoke line trailing up through the opening in the roof.

Feeling warm and safe, I had almost dozed off. Then, Sewana began to speak.

"The trail you were on," she said, "was not the one we use for herb hunting or the one for beaver."

"I have never gone that way before," I told her.

"This one begins deep inside the forest." She spoke low as though she was revealing a forbidden secret. "Only deer and other wild animals know of it for it is well hidden. Many times it turns in circles then bends here and there. Never is it a straight line. The journey has its end at a long, mountainous rock wall, sacred to the Indian. At the top there is a cave. There you will find an Indian burial ground. To get to this you must climb the rock. I will walk that trail only at the end of life. There is a tree that tells the direction to go. Indians call it 'Bent Tree.' It is the sign that points the way to the sacred rock. Its roots are deep, its trunk sturdy. The middle of the trunk bent long ago and held its curve against the ground. Later it reached for the sky again. This was the tree that sheltered you from the storm."

"But how did the wolves find that trail?" I asked.

"They know a deer scent from miles," she said. "They followed that doe along the Bent Tree trail."

Heavy winds and driving snow continued on and off for several months. Staying within the hut was making me more and more restless. Ever since my dream at the Bent Tree, thoughts of North Dakota had been entering my head more and more. Pictures of my family and old memories of home flashed through my mind. Time moved slowly in those months. There were still the animals to care for, but there was more quiet time than my body was used to.

Because of gathering plants in summer and fall, we had plenty of food in the hut and only ventured out when the sky was sunny. Then, we'd set traps for birds and rabbit and were successful most of the time. Those were the nights our meals were prepared with fresh meat, a welcome change for my stomach and Sewana's.

The wolves were gone most mornings, on the hunt again. It became too difficult to follow them for the snow was deep, in most places over the high tops of my winter moccasins. The four must have succeeded in their search for food for they always seemed satisfied when they returned to the hut. On the days they hung around home I figured their bellies were full from a larger kill. Otherwise, they were out every day if it only meant catching a mouse or rabbit.

At times the three still acted like pups, loving to play with me in the snow. They'd dig their noses under the drifts then jump up when I came near and run around me in circles. It was their idea of hide-and-go-seek. I'd throw snowballs and they'd try to catch them, shaking their heads when the ball of snow collapsed in their mouths. Strong One never entered in these games, simply sitting by the hut while we played.

One evening after Minya, Wahya, Minsun, and Strong One had been gone all day, Sewana and I were sitting by the fire pit when we heard them return. I lifted the door hide to greet them and was shocked by what I saw. Dropped on the snow in front of me was the leg of a deer. All four wolves stood tall, proud as could be, their tails wagging.

Sewana came to the door. "Well," she said, "they have brought home a part of their hunt. They must think of this place as their den. They are honoring us as part of the pack."

"I can't believe they didn't eat it," I said.

"Or save it. They will store food when they cannot eat it all, dig a hole and hide it. When they are hungry, they find it. This time they brought it to us."

My wolves! I smiled. They think of us as part of their pack.

We took the meat inside. It was still fresh. Sewana immediately began to cut it into small pieces and trim off the fat. She put water and salt into one of her largest bowls, dropped in the meat, and covered it with a lid.

"Sitting in the liquid overnight will make it tender," she said.

The next day, while the meat was cooking, she made the fry bread I loved, something to soak up the juices. Every once in a while, she would lift the bowl cover, add more water, and stir. The smells floated around the room, making it difficult to wait for dinner. We kept the wolves outside the hut while the meat cooked as the odor inside might send them into a frenzy.

That night we filled our stomachs with deer meat. We felt as satisfied as the wolves must have felt when they had eaten their fill. Whatever leftovers we had were placed outside the hut for our "pack." The next morning there wasn't a scrap left.

We were fully prepared for the winter season with foods that would sustain us through the snow and cold. We had smoked and dried meat from the animals we trapped and stored it away in lidded pots. Any fur pelts we had were cleaned, plied until soft, then sewn into clothing for the future. Some would be used to cover and insulate the hut. Nothing was wasted. Every part of the animal was used for something. It was a constant effort—drying food, dealing with pelts, taking care of the wolves.

While the job was tiring, it was during these long hours working side by side that Sewana and I shared stories, learning more and more about each other.

"How did you find me on the prairie? How did you know about 'Ned?'" I asked her one day while tying herbs together to hang in the hut.

"I did not know him. Words traveled from tribe to tribe that a man lived alone on the prairie... a dangerous man... one who killed for pleasure. One who drank spirits until he slept long then went out to kill again. 'Stay away,' we were warned."

"Who warned you?" I asked.

"At times I have taken herbs to the Shaman who is now healer for many tribes. From him I heard of this man. When I go to the prairie, I have seen this man's traps in the forest. The animals of the forest live free and only take what they need to survive. He takes what he does not need. He kills because he can. He should not do that." Sewana continued to work with the dried plants as we talked, her forehead a frown.

"The day of the sand-wind I had been on the prairie. I saw you standing on the mound of the coulee. I had seen you many times before at the cistern. Saw the scars from when he beat you. I brought you here, far from the prairie, hidden now in these mountains. He will not find us."

Her words brought back thoughts of my first months on the prairie, of my hope of finding homestead land for my father, of being a captive at the dugout and of the inhumane treatment from ol' "Ned." So, I began to talk of Streeter and of my father and mother. My sister. I had already shown Sewana the picture of my family that I had in my poncho pocket when she rescued me from the sandstorm.

I said, "Being gone for so long, first in the dugout with 'Ned,' then in these mountains, I know that my family has worried themselves sick and certainly would have begun to search for me months ago. They had been ready to come west and claim land. But I have been gone for so long without even a word, I sometimes wonder... if they might have given up."

I said, "It was not possible for me to send my father a letter when I lived with 'Ned.' He would never have helped me. I had no idea where I was on that open prairie or from which direction I had come. I didn't dare leave. Each day I had become weaker from not having enough to eat or from being worked until I could barely stand and from having been thrashed until I bled. Then you rescued me. You were kind, patient, watching over me while I slowly gained back my strength. While I healed, you taught me how to search for herbs, how to hunt, how to appreciate the forest and what it gave. Then, just as I felt I was strong enough to leave, we found the pups. I wanted to care for them, keep them safe, and prepare them to survive on their own."

As I said these things, I could feel my heart swell with gratitude for my time in the forest with Sewana. Yet my mind kept taking me away to my family. I had begun to see their faces clearly again, remember tender moments in Streeter. I loved it here, but I wanted to go home more than ever. Then I heard myself say, "I must go home. Find my family. Did they leave Streeter? Did they go west to Ruff? I must go!! But I don't know my way. I need you to show me."

Sewana was quiet for a while. "You cannot go now. It is a long way," she said. "I might have taken you to the prairie a while ago, before the leaves began to color, but you were not strong enough. The gathering, the hunting... all this I wanted you to know when you left so you would not go hungry. And the pups... they needed you. Now... the winter. The storms have closed in. Soon more great snows will come. I must teach you to look for the smallest insects, for worms to eat. With these too you will not go hungry. You must have all knowledge of how to go on alone. All this first. Then you may leave."

Sewana was right. Before I left, I still had much to learn for my own survival.

Though I desperately wanted to leave, I was torn. Having spent the past seasons with Sewana, she had become like family. But forced by the weather to remain in the hut, I began to notice things... things I hadn't noticed earlier. I could see that each day her body bent more and more, her steps slowed, her sleep was restless. Her hands trembled as she removed the stew pot from the fire pit. When I tried to help, she would brush me away. Surely she knew that her body was weakening but, if so, kept it to herself.

The season moved along, snow becoming much too deep to walk through in winter moccasins without sinking to our knees. One morning Sewana went to the hut's lean-to, returning with two pairs of snowshoes.

I was fascinated by how they had been made. A bent-branch holder, shaped like a teardrop, crossed at the ends and tied with sinew. Smaller branches went down and across the curve then were tied.

"Put these on." Sewana held a pair out to me. "Give them a try. The wolves have pads on their paws to keep them atop the drifts. These are like that. They will help you move about easily."

I had never needed to use snowshoes in Streeter, where the snow was never deep enough not to trudge through with boots. Laying these on the hut floor, I stood on one to check its size. I found the contraption fit perfectly though it felt a bit awkward. Near the crosspiece at the front was an extra strip of strong long sinew. "Take this piece. Run it through the laces on your moccasins. Tie it to the other side of the snowshoe base." Sewana bent to help me.

I did that and began to flop around the room with only the one snowshoe on, the other foot still in a moccasin. Sewana was laughing. "Now put the other one on. Walk outside. Give them a try."

It was difficult moving about the hut at first, accidently catching one snowshoe on my deerskin blanket then stumbling through the door. The wolves stood around outside, barking at me in a tone that sounded like laughter as I tried out this new way of walking.

It didn't take me long—just a couple of tumbles sideways before I found the fun of being able to move in a slow-motion gallop on top of the snow without sinking. From then on it was easy to travel some distances without tiring from the exertion of trying to move through deep drifts.

I could barely wait to get up in the morning, put on those snowshoes, go out to check snares or just have fun walking through the forest. The more I moved about, the more quickly I could cover the snowy ground. Sewana often went with me, and if the wolves were around they'd follow.

LATE WINTER 1905

FTER A TIME, WHEN I thought spring was surely
getting closer, a surprise rogue storm would
come and dump a few more inches of snow. In
between, the sun would shine and its warmth would melt
the new snow quickly. These late winter storms didn't last
for more than part of a day.

When the wind would finally stop its howling, we
always knew the worst was over for the time being. Then
the temperature would rise a bit, the sky would be the
brilliant blue that winter brings, and the forest would
be alive with the sound of melting snow falling from
branches and dripping from icicles. The wolves would
rise from their den behind the hut, creating their own
miniature storm, snow pillowing off their fur as they
shook themselves awake.

The winter season was passing quickly, and I could
almost begin to smell the smells that wet earth brings

with spring. In some of the hidden places among the forest pines, where sun had pinpointed small patches of already melting snow, tiny green shoots of an unknown plant would be seen. Still the deeper forest had a depth of white that could often only be crossed when using snowshoes. I was told by Sewana that this winter had been mild, not nearly as much snow had fallen as in past years.

Early one morning I went out to check the snares on my own, returning late afternoon. The wolves were gone, their tracks leading into the forest. When I entered the hut Sewana was not there. I began to boil water and prepare a meal so that she could rest when she returned, but, being hungry after the long day, I ate mine and set hers aside. Then, though trying to stay awake, I fell asleep and did not awaken until it was dark. The wolves had already come home and had settled down outside.

But where was Sewana!

Then the night noises caught up to me and I began to worry. Should I search for her? But how was I to see in the darkness? There was no moon, there were no stars, the sky having been covered all day by thick blankets of threatening clouds. What if another storm came and she was out there alone?

"She will be fine," I told myself. "After all, she taught me how to survive."

But she had become more frail. What if she had fallen, been attacked... what if... my thoughts went back and forth.

That night, nothing. Sewana did not return. I lay there, now and then drifting into a worrisome dream then awakening, alert to any sound in the hut or the forest beyond. The instant dawn came, I jumped up, dressed, packed a pack and left the hut. The wolves stood to greet me, shaking the dampness from their fur.

Because the snow by the hut was slowly melting, prints from paws, snowshoes, and winter moccasins wove together, so there was no clear impression of any kind. There would be no tracks to lead me. No easy clue as to where she had gone.

At first I thought of our gathering and hunting spots, and, with the wolves beside me, walked in that direction. But finding nothing, my mind kept coming back to the place Sewana had described: the trailhead that lay below our hut, winding miles back up the mountain and ending at the base of the rocky outcrop where the wolves had cornered the deer. And so, I decided to change direction, descend the mountain, and find that trailhead.

Because it would mean many days of travel, I returned to the hut and hurriedly gathered food and gear. Then, carrying the bundle outside, I went to the lean-to. Since the animals would be left alone for some time while we searched for Sewana, they had to have food and water.

I moved aside the interlocking tree boughs that closed off the front of the lean-to. The goat roamed free inside while several chickens sat in nesting boxes that pressed against the warmer side portion of the hut. I overloaded the hens' feed box with seeds, then covered the floor of the shelter with dried thistle and dandelion leaves and grain and pine needles for the goat. The trough—a hollowed out log—was already filled with water, which had never frozen solid because of its closeness to the warm hut.

When I was satisfied all the animals would be able to survive until I returned, I put a rope around Kamali's neck and led her out of the space, resetting the boughs behind me. I had decided to take her along. If Sewana was in trouble, had fallen or worse, she could ride on the pony's back. I would carry the woven pack of food and supplies.

The wolves had been following me around since dawn, instinctively knowing something about this day was troubling. At first I was going to leave them behind. Then I thought of their scent training and how good they were at playing that game when they were pups. I was certain they would be a great help in finding Sewana. Besides, I knew they would never let me leave without them.

We began our tracking—Kamali, Minya, Wahya, Minsun, Strong One, and me.

Kamali's legs were steady and strong. She seemed to know how to navigate the path. We took it slow, always aware of what was around us, looking for some clue that Sewana had actually come this way.

The wolves kept sniffing the fallen branches and ground. Melting snow had made the trail slushy, forming puddles in places where the sun came streaming through the trees. They spent time dipping their noses near the water then raising them to the wind. Often they zigzagged off the path out of my sight for a short time.

The trail was not an easy one. Though it led downhill, there were steep turns, rocks, narrow cliff overhangs, tangles of fallen trees, any number of things that we had to go around or through. As we walked, I made small notches in the trees so that I might find my way back.

I was seeing this part of the forest for the first time, so I knew nothing of the path we had chosen or how long it would be until we reached our destination, if in fact we ever did. Except for the wolves' continuous forward tracking, nothing else gave me hope that Sewana had gone along this dense trail.

By night the ground had leveled off, so we stopped and sheltered under a clump of evergreens. I tied Kamali's rope to a tree stump, laid some pine boughs on the ground, and settled down with my wolves beside me. After a few bites of dried meat I was asleep.

My dreams were strong: a frozen country where I was searching, pushing forward, the wolves by my side. I clearly saw Sewana, grey hair pulled back in a single braid, her blue eyes, her gentle smile, standing in the meadow, moving toward the forest. But then her eyes were no longer open and she was no longer standing but instead lay on the damp ground. I awoke crying out, "Find her. Find her!"

The wolves had risen from their sleep perhaps awakened by my calling out. Where they had slept the ground had been flattened by their body weight. I noticed their bellies were more rounded than the previous day and knew that during the night they must have left to hunt.

Early morning brought more sunshine. Kamali had been pawing the melting snow, uncovering spring grass and plants that had just begun to peek through. I untied her rope from the tree stump and let her graze close to us while I prepared to leave our overnight spot.

The wolves began to trot ahead of me, zigzagging deeper into the trees. They'd run ahead, return to me, then take off again. It was difficult to follow them since I was leading Kamali through bent and broken boughs that had crowded the forest floor during the winter storms. This went on until midday where, deep into the woods, we began to go downhill again.

The four had their noses to the ground and were moving quickly. I was listening for any sound that might mean Sewana was near, but the slight whisper of mist as it fell into the melting snow puddles was all that could be heard. Mist soon became rain, gentle at first, then a collection of drops. There was no wind. A certain scent on the dirt, new grass and plant shoots, must have been strong for the wolves were anxiously moving in starts and stops every few moments.

As quickly as it had come, the rain stopped and the mist returned. Slowly, sunlight came through the treetops, making the earth and wet tree branches glisten. We walked on, the pony and I trailing behind the wolves.

When we first saw the tracks, they looked as though they might have been made by winter moccasins. The slush, mud, and melted snow had mostly filled in the prints so it was difficult to tell. By now we were long gone from the hut and any familiar trail, but I continued hoping we were on the right path. Suddenly Strong One sprang forward. The others watched for a moment, then took off after him. I pulled Kamali ahead, leading her through clumps of pine that finally opened onto a small cluster of berry bushes. Ahead of me, all four wolves were sitting on their haunches and had begun to whine and howl.

I let Kamali's lead rope go, hurried over to them, and went down on my knees. Pushing aside the twisted limbs as best as I could, I could see, hidden within the bushes, Sewana's body lying on its side, legs bent, arms tightly wrapped around her knees.

Kamali nickered. The wolves stood and began circling, sniffing, pushing their noses against me as I pulled at the branches to make a shallow tunnel.

"Sewana," I said, relieved. She stared at me, not seeming to know who I was.

"Sewana!" I said again, and with that she reached out and took hold of my arm.

"I have fallen." Her voice was a strained whisper.

As I looked around to see what might have caused her to fall, the bright sunrays now streaming through the trees bounced off a shiny object half covered in a shallow drift. Taking a branch, I slowly scraped away the melting snow. Hidden beneath—a wolf trap, its sharp jaws open, waiting to snap shut.

"She must have tripped over the staked chain that connects to the trap," I thought.

I leaned in carefully, put my arms under Sewana's body, then slowly slid her from under the bushes. Picking up a fallen branch, I sprang the trap.

The wet ground and rain that had fallen had soaked her hair and run down the neck of her deerskin clothing. She was shivering in the damp air. With my help she stood but then instantly fell against my side. I sat her against the trunk of a nearby pine, took the blanket from Kamali's back, and wrapped it around her trembling body. It was important to get her warmed.

The wolves surrounded us wanting to be as close to her as possible. They licked her face, leaned their weight against her and would not leave her alone. Strong One would barely let me tend to her.

"Are you hurting?" I asked.

She shook her head. "No." But I could see that something was not right.

That night we stayed where we were. I made a bed of pine needles so Sewana could rest then built a fire to prepare a meal and keep us warm. The wolves lay next to her, their body heat warming her during the night.

When we awoke the next morning, I prepared a quick meal and cleaned up the camp area. When all was ready, I set Sewana on Kamali's back. While I had grown stronger and taller during my seasons with her, she had become smaller, thinner, more the size of my younger sister in Streeter, so it was easy to lift her.

I wrapped a rope around Kamali's neck, made a slipknot, then placed the loose ends into Sewana's left hand. Straddling the pony, she leaned forward and with her right hand gripped the mane. The three pups watched our every move while Strong One circled the pony, whining, seemingly concerned about Sewana.

Using the corner of the rope as a lead, we began our ascent through the forest. It would be easier to return to the hut now for this time the knife notches I had made in the forest trees would help us find our way.

Kamali would have to be led carefully. Though sure-footed, if she stumbled, Sewana could lose her balance, fall under Kamali's belly, and be trampled. But the pony moved forward as gently as possible, seeming to sense the importance of carrying the weakened Indian woman on her back.

The next day was clear, light shining through the forest branches. By nightfall we had come upon a patch in the woods where a grassy area had been warmed and dried by the sun. Here we would spend our second night.

This time I made a bed of soft grasses near the tree line then lifted Sewana off the pony. When I set her down she moaned and reached for her foot.

Removing the moccasin was difficult. Once it was off, I saw that her ankle was badly swollen and bruised, but there were no broken bones that I could feel. Dipping strips of rag from my woven pack in a cold puddle of melted snow, I wrapped them around the injury, keeping it in place with sinew.

Sewana's eyes were closed, and, because her body shuddered now and then, I felt it was important to build a warm fire and shelter as quickly as I could. Kamali had begun grazing. The wolves were moving in and out of the trees, encircling the cleared area as if checking to see that everything was safe. I stepped into the edge of the woods where fallen limbs were plentiful and could be used to build a small shelter and where kindling and dried grass could be gathered to make a fire. The simple shelter of tree limbs would protect her; the fire would keep her warm.

That night we ate dried fruit, seeds, and strips of smoked deer meat that I had brought in my pack. The stars looked down from the sky, the fire burned with a steady orange-blue glow. It wasn't long before Sewana fell into a fitful sleep. Though her hair was now dry and her body warmed by the blanket, the bodies of the wolves, and the fire, she still shivered.

I slept in the open, close to the fire. When I got up to add more wood, I noticed that the three pups were gone. Only Strong One was lying nearby, eyes open, alert. Each time I awoke he was there guarding our camp or with his body pressed against Sewana. Kamali too stayed near grazing, her ears flicking now and then, her muzzle blowing out puffs of air in the cool night. It seemed she too was on guard.

As each day passed, we moved closer to the hut. Sewana seemed to be getting weaker and would only take a small amount of food and water. She had begun to fall asleep while riding, her head nodding. At times, while still keeping her knees tight against Kamali's belly for balance, her upper body would fall forward, her cheek against the horse's neck. Even then she still held tightly to the rope and mane. She didn't speak on the ride, only mumbled a sing-song chant now and then—one I could barely hear. She had begun to cough, the heaviness increasing as we went along.

By day we moved forward. At night, rested. We were lucky the weather had become warmer and was sunny. The earth smelled of spring. Grasses and weeds were popping up everywhere. When we finally reached the hut, I lifted Sewana off the pony, brought her inside, placed her on a deerskin bed and covered her with a blanket. She leaned back and fell asleep immediately.

SPRING 1905

No matter what I did, Sewana did not seem to improve. Her cough sounded strained, her skin paled, her cheeks became sunken. She ate less and less and only drank small amounts of water. A fever would come and go. Sweat soaked her body. There was a look in her eyes that said she was thinking of something far away and long past. When she talked (which was seldom) she talked only of me.

"Spring," she said one day, her voice weak. "Winter has passed. It is time for you to leave... go home. I have taught you what I could, and you have learned well. Knowing what we have been given... animals, plants... all that is on this earth will remain with you. Choose wisely. Lead with your heart. Teach others. The Spirits will provide and protect you. Go home."

While I had heard those words even in my dreams, Sewana's illness was more important to me at that moment. I had to see that she got well again before I could even imagine leaving. But each day she seemed to become more frail. When awake she would sing the same chant she had mumbled on the trail, then after she would tell me how to face the world that was soon to come.

"The enemy is close," she said one morning. "That is why I went to the trailhead. My heart told me he was near... the killer of animals without reason. A man who destroys, hurts others. You must leave soon. You have marked the trees to where you found me. Continue from there and you will come to the trailhead. It is a long journey. The wolves have grown enough now to live on their own. Strong One will lead them. Leave all behind. Take Kamali. I give her to you."

Tears worked their way up from my insides, choked my throat, clouded my eyes, and spilled down my cheeks. I had spent the year with Sewana. Learned the gentleness of her ways. All that she had taught me. How she loved the animals, the woods. I had come to think of her not only as a healer and seer of what was to come but as family.

That night I rose once to keep the fire going. Sewana's cough had stopped, so I slept more peacefully, soothed by the sounds of the night.

Before dawn I dressed and started to boil water. The hut was still. Morning light had not yet crept through the door. Though the fire had burned low, I could still see the circular room in its glow. I looked over toward where Sewana slept. The low fire was causing strange shapes to move about the floor and walls of the hut. At first I thought I saw her lying there, tossing a bit in her sleep. But as I looked more closely, I knew the shadows made by the fire were fooling me. Her bed was empty.

I donned my warmer outer clothing then went outside to the lean-to. Only Kamali, the goat, and the hens were there. The wolves were nowhere to be seen. I began to climb upward toward the meadow. It was a while before I reached the spot, but she was not there. I turned back to the hut. My instinct told me to go from there to the bent tree several miles away, perhaps even farther to the barrier of rock that she had said contained the cave.

Where had she gone? She was sick and needed care. My heart pounded. Quickly I stuffed a pack with food and water then plunged through the woods toward the place I had spent the winter storm that night several months before. I moved as fast as possible, cautious around fallen tree limbs and patches of muddied earth.

Though the morning had been sunny, a slight breeze had come up and clouds had begun to form overhead. From the bent tree to the rock barrier would still be several more miles. Ferns had begun to grow, their curled fronds ready to open. Moss lay slippery with dew on the ground and rocks. Everything seemed fresh, ready to burst with life, but I didn't stop to enjoy the newness. The sky was quickly filling with more and more clouds, each swollen, each with a dark flat base.

I reached the bent tree and moved on, anxious to reach the mountainous rock that held the cave Sewana had told me about. The sky had become murky and threatening. Within a mile, the rain began, a downpour that included pelts of ice. I pulled the hood of my deerskin coat over my head to protect myself and trudged on.

It was a while before I came to the rock. The mountainous barrier rose up in front of me. Because of the rain its cave was but a small dot above, hardly visible. I called out Sewana's name. There was no answer, no sound other than threatening thunder from the storm around us.

"I must climb," I thought. "But how?"

The length of the wall covered a huge area, the height tall and sheer. I walked along the front but there was no way of attaching a rope and climbing to the cave opening above. I walked to a section of the mammoth structure then sat, put my head in my hands, and tried to think. "There must be a way. Sewana had said this was an Indian burial site, so others must have climbed here." I leaned against the rock.

That's when I felt a sharp edge poke against my back. I stood, turned, and saw that my body had been pressed against a vertical narrow crack, a fissure, going straight up toward an opening far above where I stood. Jutting out within the thin opening were small pieces of rock, barely visible, one above another. Right in front of me was the way to the cave above.

Shouldering my pack, I began to climb, setting my feet on the holds and using my hands to grip the one above. The steps were tilted ever so slightly, so, by leaning in toward the wall a bit, I had less fear of falling. It was not an easy climb. I never looked down, thinking I might not continue on if I did.

When I reached the level of the rock opening, I had to crawl along a thin ledge that led inside the mountain. The air outside had been cooled by the rain, but I found

I was sweating. It was late afternoon, and the cave was almost dark inside. I called Sewana's name but there was no answer, just an echo from far back in the rock.

Outside the rain had stopped and the sun had begun to send thin early evening rays through the trees. I was aware suddenly of light coming in from a hole no bigger than a pine knot in the ceiling. It settled on the floor where I stood, lighting up the space around me. Within the soft light Sewana lay on a raised platform of flat rock. She was dressed in her finest deerskin clothing. Her eyes were closed, her braided hair laying to one side of her face. She seemed younger, peaceful, the lines on her skin hardly visible. In her hands she held an eagle feather whose barb and fringe were painted delicately with white butterflies.

On the floor around the platform were several jugs, the type that held special herbs and medicines. The peace pipe we had used to feed the wolf pups lay at her feet. There was a blanket, one I had not seen before, covering her lower body. Sewana must have prepared her place in this burial cave. She had come alone knowing it was her time to leave this world.

I knelt on the floor beside her and leaned my forehead against the flat rock that held her body. I heard myself saying the prayers I had been taught by my family in

Streeter. Tears came from deep inside me and my cries echoed along the cave walls.

When I finally stood, the light from above had angled and I now could see the open space around me more clearly. Along the walls were several raised stone platforms. Animal skins covered these. Scattered around each were old clay pots and jars. It seemed many others had come here long ago at the end of their lives.

That night I slept leaning against Sewana's burial platform. When morning came I knelt and placed my head against the flattened rock again. Speaking aloud, I told of how she had saved me on the prairie, of her kindness, of her care for the earth and its animals. I wanted her to know how much she meant to me. When I finally arose and prepared to leave the cave, I knew, then, that I was leaving part of myself behind.

An eerie light had entered the front of the cave. The sky outside was again cloud covered. A strong wind had just begun. What at first I thought of as the noise of tree branches rubbing together I suddenly realized was a different sound—a sound I knew well—a horse's hooves against the ground. Then a nicker.

I slid to one side of the cave. Surely no one but tribal people could know of this place. It was so well hidden. I snaked forward on my belly and peeked over the edge. Below, a man, bearded and thin, sat upon an old horse at the base of the barrier. He was looking up toward the cave opening. I slithered backwards, out of sight.

"I see you boy!" came a booming voice. My entire body began to tremble.

"Get out here or I'll come up an' get ya. Hear me now? If'n I have to go up there it'll go worse for ya. Hear me, boy?" His voice, loud and threatening, slurred.

I moved a little closer to the opening and saw him lift a canteen to his lips—"Ned!"

"Told ya to get on down. Ain't got all day. Got wolves ta kill, pelts ta clean. Hurry it up, boy."

Then I heard a horse cry out. I crawled to the overhang again and looked down.

Because of the noise of the wind in the trees, the horse must have shied, jerking hard to one side. He was pawing the ground with one hoof. "Ned" had fallen off and was lying on a pile of leaf-covered rocks below me. He got up slowly, stumbled over to where the frightened animal stood, then punched him hard in his soft nose. The horse screamed and reared, dumping a rusted wolf trap that had been strapped loosely on his back to the ground.

"Ned" grabbed the trap by its chain and walked to the base of the rock. "You get down here now or I'm gonna knock you silly with this here thing!" he roared.

He started swinging the long chain with its trap over his head like a lasso. He was clumsy at first, the entire contraption landing on the ground once or twice. Then he got used to handling it.

I realized as I watched that the trap's chain was particularly long, not long enough to reach the cave's ledge but long enough to go a good way up the rock. Now he was using it as a weapon to get to me.

The more he swung the trap, the better he got. Then suddenly, with the force of a giant, he let the chain fly forward from his arm. The rusted trap lunged against the wall below me, making a sound that exploded through the cave and forest, and then, a giant crack. The massive rock began to spew from its top and sides. Boulders jarred loose from above, crashed down, smashing against each other, hitting the cave ledge and causing it to crumble with a thunderous crash to the earth below. The noise was deafening. Over it all I heard a horse bellow and a man's piercing scream.

At the same time, rain came in torrents. Cold air followed. Heavy winds were slamming everything imaginable against the ground. I heard hail. I pulled back into the cave far enough that I felt safe but could still see the opening. It seemed the whole world was collapsing around me. The sky above spit all it had with a blast that left me shaking.

From the top of the massive rock came a rumbling noise like that of a thousand stampeding horses. Huge trees, yanked from their roots by the storm, pitched past the cave opening. Branches, bushes, dirt, rocks, whatever had been torn from the earth, cascaded down. The entire mountain seemed to be folding in on itself. The fury of the storm had only taken several minutes, its force crashing relentlessly into the earth.

Then, everything became still. The forest lay deadly quiet as if nothing had happened only seconds before. Nothing moved. Not animal or bird. The whinny of the horse and the voice of the man had been silenced.

Now only a gentle rain remained.

I stood where the ledge had once been and looked below. Piles of trees, branches, rocks, and whatever had been in the path of that forceful wind and hail, covered the forest floor, reaching up as far as the cave opening. A half-mile width of destruction lay spread before me, its downward path continuing as far as my eyes could see. Yet the forest on either side still stood, having never been touched. I walked back a few paces, picked up my pack, and hung it around my neck. The ledge was now gone and there was no way I could crawl back to the fissure and climb down. With the ruins of the storm having risen to the cave floor, this could be my way out. It would be a dangerous descent, certainly, but my only real chance to leave.

Several branches had shoved their way into the opening of the cave, jabbing my body as I moved to look down. The trunk of one tree was braced against the rock wall. Other debris lay under, against, and on all sides of it. I pulled at the branches to see if anything gave way. They swayed a bit, but the trunk held firm.

I moved out of the opening, extending one leg onto a limb while gripping the branch above with my hands. Reaching with the other leg, I found a branch directly below. Moving each hand then each leg, I used the tree's limbs as I would stair steps. At times I stopped, afraid of falling, being cut, breaking bones. Then I remembered the many times I had climbed trees as a boy in Streeter. I was determined then. I would be now.

Slowly, over and over, I made the same move until I reached the enormous roots, the torn base that had once bound the tree to the earth. The debris would be another challenge. Piled high with branches, bushes, rock, it looked as if it would fall even farther down the sloop if slightly touched.

Where to step first was the question. It was like a game of pick-up-sticks. If I moved one piece, it would jar another and I would lose. Gently I reached one leg out and let my foot touch the very edge of the entwined pieces. Everything shifted instantly, falling down the hill. Surely, I would tumble along with it if I left this spot.

And then I saw a flash of white. The rain had almost stopped, and the sun was coming out. At first I thought it must be the rays reflecting off remaining drops. The white flash grew closer until it swirled in the air around and above me. After a moment it dipped in a line that extended beyond the debris to a distant stand of pine that stood tall and untouched. Tiny wings stroked the air making soft soothing sounds. Hundreds hovered directly over the fallen trees and twisted branches that lay around me. Butterflies! White butterflies!!

I reached out a foot, carefully putting weight on the pile and found, though it gave a little, this time it didn't shift.

So, I took a chance and slowly lowered myself. Guarding against even the slightest movement, I maneuvered my way across the storm's jumbled path, following the flight pattern of the white butterflies that flew above. They spread out toward the still standing pines in a straight line, the sun reflecting off their translucent wings.

Moving along was treacherous but I was not afraid. I was being led.

When I finally reached the pines, I felt safe at last. I sat for a while, relief filling my body and mind. Above me hundreds of white butterflies had gathered and were resting, their wings folded upward, pointing to the heavens. I looked back toward the cave then began to walk down the hill on the path to the hut. Overhead the butterflies rose to lead the way.

I followed the stand of pine that edged the path of the storm's destruction until there was no choice but to cross over it and find the trail that led to the hut.

It was after dark when I had to stop. I never even thought to make a shelter but merely lay exhausted on the ground, my pack under my head, my body huddled down inside my deerskin coat.

Dew fell heavily during the night. I awoke early feeling the dampness on my clothes and scolded myself for not having built a shelter. I ate a bit of jerky, drank some water, and started on my way again. Just as they had the day before, the white butterflies swooped from the trees above and went on ahead of me.

As I walked on I thought about my life here in these woods. About Sewana. The wolves.

"Where are the wolves?" I asked myself. "Surely they must have wondered where we had gone when they returned to the hut these past days."

Then I thought of Sewana's word. "You must leave soon. The enemy is close."

"Ned" had been close. But his death had come with the storm's violent outburst. I didn't have to fear him anymore. Now I could leave for the prairie. Find my family. But what about the wolves? "Where were they?" I asked myself again. I couldn't leave without them.

"Find the wolves. Find my family," I repeated to myself, feeling I must reach the hut soon and sort out my thoughts.

About twenty feet from the hut I saw them: Wahya, Minsun, and Strong One. They were standing in front of the lean-to. Without greeting me, they turned and walked past the bough fencing that lay in shambles on the ground. I followed. After a few moments the three stopped, muzzles pointing to something lying at their feet. It was Minya.

I knelt down and began to stroke her head, rub her ears like as I had done so many times. She lay on her side, her eyes open, looking at me. There was blood on her back and neck. The wolves closed in beside me, watching as I ran my hands over the wounds, checking to see how deep they were. The one on her back was only a surface cut. The neck wound was still bleeding and looked deep, down to the bone. It needed tending immediately.

The deerskin that had covered the door had been torn apart and lay on the ground. The inside wooden poles that supported the structure had been struck over and over with something like a chain. They listed to one side, hardly able to keep the dome roof from collapsing.

The floor was cluttered with broken jars, dried herbs, plants, and woven storage baskets twisted and torn beyond repair. Everything had been smashed or scattered—blankets, clothing, pots, pans, ashes, and wood from the fire pit. Everywhere there were depressions from a horse's hooves.

I had to hurry, find something to stitch the wound together. Sewana's closed basket of bone needles and horse-tail hair lay in the cold ashes of the fire pit. I pulled it out and found the material inside to still be usable. Grabbing that, a cloth, and a jar, I ran from the hut to the stream, then back to the yard where Wahya, Minsun, and Strong One were standing over Minya.

A fire had to be started to heat the jar of stream water. There was enough hay and sticks lying about the lean-to that could be used. I brushed aside a space on the ground so the fire would not spread then used my knife and flint to start a flame. I knelt beside Minya and began to work on her, gently massaging the skin around the neck wound so it would drain. She whimpered but lay still. The fluid was thick and discolored. "Infected," I thought. I kept massaging until at last the discharge was thin and clear. The infected part had finally drained.

When the jar of water had boiled, I removed it from the fire. After giving it a while to cool I dipped my rag into it, washed the wound, dabbing and cleansing, then poured the remaining liquid over the open sore until the jar was empty. I used the horse-tail hair and bone needle to stitch the skin together. Minya raised her head, looked at me while I worked on her, but then lay back.

After, I went to the stream, brought back water, held her head and let her drink. She slept then, the three wolves by her side.

In the confusion I hadn't noticed that Kamali, the goat, and the hens were gone. All around the yard were clumps of chicken feathers. I hoped the pony and goat had not become prey too but had escaped through the broken bough barrier and were safe somewhere in the woods. Later I would hunt the forest for them, but at the moment my mind was occupied with Minya.

I had thought that, having found the wolves, I could leave for the prairie, take them with me, try to find my family. But now I was again held back. Minya had to be cared for until the danger of infection had past and she was strong enough to move. So, I set up camp outside the lean-to, ate and slept there, and watched over her.

The three wolves left at dusk every day, bringing back part of their hunt for Minya. I cooked some of their kill for myself in pots from the hut's wreckage. All the while the white butterflies rested in trees above the hut while I waited for the perfect time to depart.

One morning I had gone into the forest to gather pine sap, an Indian remedy to sooth and heal wounds. I was close to the beaver pond. A deer was drinking by the water's edge.

The animal raised it head. It had wheat-colored skin with a print of white here and there... a white butterfly shape on its flank... this was not a deer. It was Kamali!

I walked toward the pony, both arms extended.

She raised her head, her ears flicking, and pressed her nose against my palms. I began to stroke her neck. She nuzzled her head into my shirt. While we stood like this, I wrapped my arms around her neck and sobbed, overcome by my memories.

Minya gathered her strength back rapidly, eating ravenously and drinking water. She healed more quickly than expected until she was able to run as if she had never been hurt. During our stay by the lean-to, each day had become warmer and in the forest the snow had almost completely melted. The longer the time went on, the more impatient I became to leave and find my way to the prairie. I judged we would soon be ready, and one bright, sky-blue morning we were.

I took my pack, looked back once, then, along with Kamali and the wolves, headed down the trail to where, weeks before, we had found Sewana. The notches I had made in the trees were still there. The way was clear to me.

For several days we walked, camped at night, made shelters, ate, and rested until we reached the spot where Sewana had encountered the wolf trap. Beyond this point the forest became a mystery. I had never gone any farther. It would be up to me to find the trailhead where Sewana and I had first ridden into the forest on the back of her pony four seasons ago.

The section of forest I had lived in with Sewana had become completely familiar to me. I knew the way to the meadow, to the pond and stream, and on up to the mountain. I knew where to find herbs and where to hunt. But now, not knowing where we were or how far we still had to travel, I felt lost. Yet I still had to hold on to the belief that we would eventually reach the trailhead.

For many days we trudged on, not knowing for certain where we were, needing to trust in the purposeful flight of the white butterflies that flew above us. As we walked, the forest began to change. Trees were thinning out. More and more boulders spread over the ground. We were moving on at a steady downhill pace.

Then one morning—there it was, a brilliant light, nothing blocking it, not a tree, not a mountain. Sunrays were streaming through an opening at the edge of the forest. I walked forward with Kamali and the wolves. The butterflies hovered above. Here was the trailhead at last, the place Sewana and I had entered on her pony, racing to escape the sandstorm and "Ned." Behind us was the forest, the uphill stretch she and I had galloped through. Before me lay a vast prairie. I sat for a moment, looking out at the waving grasses and clumps of sagebrush.

I had come back almost to the beginning.

"Where to now?" I wondered. The butterflies hung in the air above me but did not fly out into the open. Wahya, Minya, and Minsun lay down. Strong One stood beside them.

I led Kamali and moved out onto the prairie, expecting the wolves to follow. I looked back to where they lay at the edge of the space that led to the forest beyond. I whistled and called their names again and again. But they stayed where they were.

"I can't leave them! They are mine! They belong to me!" I shouted to the heavens.

That's when I knew. They would never come. They were a part of the mountains, the forest, the streams and ponds. I put my forehead against Kamali's neck and wept for what had been. The time had come for me to walk on without them, unclear of what lay ahead.

It was morning when Kamali and I began traveling over the prairie. The temperature was comfortable, the wind slight. My thoughts were on my mother, father, sister, and home. All I carried with me was the pack that held supplies. The clothes I wore were of deerskin. My hair had not been cut in a year. I had grown some. I didn't look like my old self.

"When I find them will they recognize me?" I wondered, thinking of my family. When! It was always a question of when, never if.

About halfway through the day I came across a coulee. It held a small amount of water from early spring snow run-off. Kamali and I stopped. I let her drink while I bathed. At least I would be clean when I saw my family.

Standing there I remembered having hidden in just such a coulee cave the year before when I escaped from "Ned." I walked along its edge where other small openings existed. None were big enough for me to hide in, but as I walked, they became bigger until one seemed like a good size for a boy needing a hiding place.

I bent down and tried to slip inside, but my body had grown enough over the past year that I couldn't quite fit, so I peeked into the cave instead. As my eyes grew accustomed to the dark, I saw some kind of animal had made its home in one corner. Though I struggled to shove my body forward for a better look, there was no way I could get my shoulders into the space. But something told me that whatever was in this cave belonged to me. I pushed my head and neck inside as far as I could. My eyes adjusted to the semi-darkness. That's when I realized what I was seeing.

This was the very cave I had chosen as my hiding spot after escaping from the dugout. What my eyes saw in the corner was my journal, the one I had carried all the way from Streeter, North Dakota. Stretching my arms as far as they would go, I was able to grab a part of its fabric cover and pull it toward me. Pushing backward until I was clear of the opening, I leaned against the entrance.

The journal cover was dry. It seemed water from other parts of the coulee had never risen high enough to seep to the back of this particular cave. I folded over page after page, reading quickly as I did. So many memories—train travel to Ruff, frightening months living with "Ned," planning for and escaping to the coulee cave—and then I realized how much more I would now have to add to my story.

Sitting there with my memories, I suddenly became aware that the sun was overhead. I waited until it moved a bit more then judged which direction I needed to go. I knew where I now stood was north of the cistern. South was where I must travel.

After about an hour of walking, I spotted a windmill. That meant water. Since I had been gone, a new windmill had been built next to the old cistern. Now I knew exactly which way to go and turned east for the mile walk to where I had lived with "Ned."

When I reached the place, the dugout was gone, the land flattened. The sagebrush that once surrounded the place had been removed. Instead, there were acres of plowed field facing me. Then, off in the distance I saw a house, a barn, a man holding the handles of a plow that was being pulled by a horse. In the yard a woman was playing with a young girl.

Kamali and I moved forward.

EPILOGUE

1974

I HAVE BEEN A Washington wheat farmer most of my
life. In Streeter, North Dakota my father was one.
Here, near Ritzville, my sons and grandsons are
farmers, continuing the tradition. I've kept a journal
filled with all that I can remember of my journey on this
earth and will pass it on to them someday.

I'm an old man now, possibly older than the medicine
woman Sewana had been when she first found me by the
coulee. Kamali has long since passed on to where she can
run through grassy meadows and drink from clear cool
streams.

For years I've sat on my porch of an evening while
thousands of stars cover the sky. Every season brings back
memories of the hut, the forest, the meadow, and the
Indian woman who was my friend and teacher.

Sometimes I hear the wolves call. Though the calls are
far away, I recognize the voices of four wolves, then see

them turn their backs and walk away, one hobbling on three legs.

My name is Jonathan Schwartz.